# Bliss

# Bliss

## KATHRYN LITTLEWOOD

KATHERINE TEGEN BOOKS
An Imprint of HarperCollins Publishers

Katherine Tegen Books is an imprint of HarperCollins Publishers.

Bliss
Copyright © 2012 by The Inkhouse

**INKHOUSE**

Interior illustrations copyright © 2012 by Erin McGuire
For information address HarperCollins Children's Books,
a division of HarperCollins Publishers, 10 East 53rd Street,
New York, NY 10022.
www.harpercollinschildrens.com

Library of Congress Cataloging-in-Publication Data
Littlewood, Kathryn.
    Bliss / Kathryn Littlewood. — 1st ed.
        p.    cm.
    Summary: Twelve-year-old Rose Bliss wants to work magic in
her family's bakery as her parents do, but when they are called away
and Rose and her siblings are left in charge, the magic goes awry
and a beautiful stranger tries to talk Rose into giving her the Bliss
Cookery Booke.
    ISBN 978-0-06-208423-1 (trade bdg.)
    [1. Bakers and bakeries—Fiction. 2. Magic—Fiction.
3. Brothers and sisters—Fiction.   4. Books and reading—Fiction.]
I. Title.
PZ7.L736472Bli   2012                                    2011019390
[Fic]—dc23                                                        CIP
                                                                    AC

Typography by Jennifer Rozbruch
12 13 14 15 16   LP/RRDH   10 9 8 7 6 5 4 3 2 1
❖
First Edition

*For Ted*

# Contents

## PROLOGUE
## *A Pinch of Magic*

*I*t was the summer Rosemary Bliss turned ten that she saw her mother fold a lightning bolt into a bowl of batter and learned—beyond the shadow of a doubt—that her parents made magic in the Bliss bakery.

It was the month the youngest Calhoun child, six-year-old Kenny, had wandered into an open relay room at the train station, touched the wrong knob, and nearly been electrocuted. The charge hadn't killed him outright. It was just powerful enough to make his hair stand on end and to land him in the hospital.

When Rose's mother, Purdy, heard about Kenny's coma, she closed the bakery, saying, "This is no time for cookies," and then she set to work in the kitchen. She couldn't be drawn away for food or sleep. Nights passed and still she worked. Rose's father, Albert, watched Rose's siblings, while Rose begged her mother to help in the kitchen. But Rose was sent to do errands instead—to town for extra flour or dark chocolate or Tahitian vanilla.

Finally, late Sunday evening, as the fiercest storm they'd had all summer lashed Calamity Falls with thunder, lightning, and heavy rain that pounded the roof like handfuls of flung gravel, Purdy made an announcement: "It's time."

"We can't leave the children," Albert said. "Not in a storm like this one."

Purdy nodded sharply. "Then I guess we have no choice but to bring them all along." She turned and shouted upstairs, "Field trip, everyone!"

Rose hiccuped with excitement as her father packed her and her brothers and baby sister into the family's minivan, along with a large mason jar made out of worn blue glass.

Wind and rain rocked the van on its wheels and almost pushed it off the road, but Albert gritted his teeth and pressed on to the barren top of Bald Man's Peak.

He parked. "Are you sure you should be doing this?" he asked his wife.

She loosened the lid on the mason jar. "Kenny is too young. I have to at least try." And then she kicked open the door and rushed out into the rain.

Rose watched her mother stagger forward into the teeth of the storm, right into the center of the clearing. She pulled the lid off and raised the jar high over her head.

That was when the lightning came.

With a blood-stopping *crack* the first bolt tore

the sky in two and came down right into the jar. The entire plateau lit up, and Rose's mother was suddenly burning bright as though she were made of light.

"Mama!" Rose cried, and surged toward the door, but Albert held her back.

"It's not ready yet!" he said. There was another crack of lighting, and another—

Afterward Rose didn't know whether she had been blinded by the light or by her tears.

"Mama!" she whimpered.

And then the van door was opening again, and her mother slid back into the car. She was soaking wet and smelled like a burning toaster, but other than that, she looked unharmed. Rose stared into the jar and saw hundreds of crackling veins of blue light flickering about.

"Get us home pronto," Purdy said. "This is the final ingredient."

Back at home, the kids were sent to bed, but Rose stayed awake in secret and watched her mother work.

Purdy stood over a metal mixing bowl filled with a smooth white batter. She carefully positioned the mason jar over the bowl and opened the lid. Little flickers of blue light poured out of the jar and zigzagged into the batter like snakes, turning the whole thing a glowing greenish color.

Purdy turned the batter with a spoon and whispered, *"Electro Correcto."* Then she poured it into a loaf pan and put it in the oven. She closed the door and, without glancing over her shoulder, said, "You should be in bed, Rosemary Bliss."

Rose didn't sleep very well that night. Her dreams were filled with lightning, with her mother glowing an electric orange and wagging a finger at her to go to bed.

In the morning, Purdy put the loaf on a plate, added a drizzle of white frosting from a pastry bag, and called to Albert, "Let's go!" She crooked a finger at Rose. "You too."

Then Rose, Purdy, and Albert went to the hospital

room where Kenny lay.

Rose didn't think he looked so bad from the outside—a little quieter than normal, a little bluer than anyone should be—but there were grim-looking machines hooked up to him, and his pulse was a weak beeping in the tiny room.

Kenny's mother looked up, saw Mrs. Bliss, and burst into tears. "It's too late for cakes, Purdy!" she said, but Rose's mother just eased a crumb between his lips.

Nothing happened for the longest time.

And then there was the faintest *gulp*.

She slid a bigger chunk into his mouth. This time, his tongue moved and there was a louder *gulp*. Then she pushed a whole mouthful in, and his jaw seemed to work of its own accord. He chewed, and swallowed, and before his eyes opened, said, "You got any milk?"

After that moment, Rose knew that the rumors were true: The baked goods from the Follow Your Bliss

Bakery actually *were* magical. And her mother and father, despite living in a small town, owning a minivan, and sometimes wearing fanny packs, were kitchen magicians.

And Rose couldn't help but ponder: *Am I going to become a kitchen magician too?*

## CHAPTER I
## *Calamity Falls*

*T*wo years later, Rose had seen her fair share of catastrophes large and small in Calamity Falls— and had watched as her parents quietly mended them all.

When old Mr. Rook began sleepwalking onto other people's lawns, Purdy made him a batch of Stone Sleep Snickerdoodles, filling one of her giant bowls with flour, brown sugar, eggs, nutmeg, and the yawn of a weasel, which Albert had painstakingly collected.

Mr. Rook never sleepwalked again.

When huge Mr. Wadsworth got trapped at the bottom of a well and the fire department couldn't manage to pull him out, Albert trapped the tail of a cloud in one of the blue mason jars, which Purdy then baked into Fluffy White Macaroons. "I hardly think this is a time for sweets, Mrs. Bliss!" Mr. Wadsworth cried when they lowered a box, "but they're *so* delicious!" He devoured two dozen. Climbing out of the well was no problem after that—he practically floated.

And when Mrs. Rizzle, the retired opera singer, found herself too hoarse to make it through the final dress rehearsal of *Oklahoma!* at the Calamity Falls Playhouse, Purdy made a Singing Gingersnap, which required that Rose go to the market for some ginger root, and that Albert go collect the song of a nightingale—which had to be done at night.

In Germany.

Albert usually didn't mind these daring adventures to collect magical ingredients—except for the time he had to collect the sting of a bee. He always brought home a little extra, and those ingredients were carefully labeled, stored in blue mason jars, and hidden in the Follow Your Bliss kitchen where no one—except someone who knew where to look—would ever find them.

Rose was the one usually sent to collect the more mundane, less dangerous ingredients—eggs, flour, milk, nuts. The only emergencies Rose ever had to deal with were caused by her three-year-old little sister.

The morning of July 13, Rose woke to the clattering of metal bowls on the tile floor of her family kitchen. It was the kind of violent, reverberating crash that would make the hair on an ordinary person's neck stand at attention. Rose just rolled her eyes.

"Rose!" her mother shouted. "Can you come down to the kitchen?"

Rose heaved herself out of bed and stumbled down the wooden staircase, still in her undershirt and flannel shorts.

The kitchen of the Bliss home also happened to be the kitchen of the Follow Your Bliss Bakery, which Rose's parents operated out of a sunny front room that faced a bustling street in Calamity Falls. Where most families had a couch and a television, the Blisses had a counter filled with pies, a cash register, and a few booths and benches for customers.

Purdy Bliss was standing in the center of the kitchen amid a wreck of spilled metal bowls, little mountains of flour, an overturned sack of sugar, and the brilliant orange yolks of a dozen cracked eggs. White cake flour was still swirling in the air like smoke.

Rose's little sister, Leigh Bliss, sat in the center of the floor with her Polaroid camera around her neck and raw egg smeared on her cheek. She smiled gleefully as she snapped a photo of the wreckage.

"Parsley Bliss," Purdy began. "You ran through this kitchen and knocked over all the ingredients for this morning's poppy muffins. You *know* that people are waiting for our poppy muffins. And now they're not going to get any."

Leigh frowned for a moment, ashamed, then grinned widely and ran out of the room. She was still too young to feel bad about anything for longer than a minute.

Purdy threw her hands up in the air and laughed. "It's a good thing she's so cute."

Rose looked with horror at the mess on the floor. "Can I help clean?"

"No, I'll get your dad to do it. *But*," Purdy ventured, handing Rose a list scrawled on the back of an envelope, "you could ride into town and pick up these ingredients." She looked again at the wreckage on the floor. "It's a bit of an emergency."

"Sure, Mom," Rose said, resigned to her fate as the family courier.

"Oh!" Purdy cried. "I almost forgot." She removed the silver chain from her neck and handed it to Rose. The chain carried what Rose always assumed was a charm, but which, on closer inspection, revealed itself to be a silver key in the shape of a tiny whisk.

"Go to the locksmith and get a copy made of this key. We're going to need it. This is very, very important, Rosemary."

Rose examined the key. It was beautiful and delicate—like a spider touching all its toes together. She'd seen her mother wearing it like a charm around her neck, but always assumed it was just another one of her mother's bizarre jewelry choices, like the butterfly brooch whose wings spanned half a foot, or the hat-shaped hat pin.

"And when you're done, you can go buy yourself a Stetson's donut. Even though I don't know why you like them. They're quite inferior."

Rose, in fact, *hated* the taste of Stetson's donuts. They were too dry and too cakey and tasted a little like cough syrup—what else could you expect from donuts served up at a place called Stetson's Donut and Automotive Repair? But buying one meant getting to drop seventy-five cents into the outstretched hand of Devin Stetson.

Devin Stetson, who was twelve like her but seemed

so much older, who sang tenor in the Calamity Falls Community Chorus, who had sandy blond hair that fell in his eyes, and who knew how to repair a torn fan belt.

Whenever he passed her in the halls at school, she found an excuse to stare at her shoes. In fact, the most she'd ever said to him in real life was *Thanks for the donut*, but in her brain they had already sped along-side the river on his moped, had made a picnic in the middle of an open field and read poetry out loud and let the long grass tickle their faces, had kissed under a streetlamp in the fall. Maybe today she would cross one of those off her list of things to do in real life with Devin Stetson. Or not. What would he want with a baker?

Rose turned to go get dressed.

"Oh, and another thing!" Purdy cried again. "Take your little brother with you."

Rose looked past the mess in the kitchen and through the side door into the yard, where her younger brother, Sage Bliss, was bouncing with gusto on their giant trampoline, shouting theatrically, still in his pajamas.

Rose groaned. Carrying ingredients in the front basket of her bike was hard enough, but dragging Sage from door to door made the whole thing ten times harder.

*1. Borzini's Nuttery. 1 lb. poppy seeds.*

Rose and Sage leaned their bikes against the stuccoed storefront of Borzini's Nuttery and went inside. You really couldn't miss Borzini's Nuttery. It was the only store in Calamity Falls shaped like a peanut.

Sage marched immediately to a barrel of Mr. Borzini's fanciest imported Ethiopian macadamia nuts, shoved his arms into the barrel, and tossed dozens of the nuts in the air. Rose stared at her brother as he scrambled like a nervous juggler to catch the macadamias in his mouth before they hit the floor.

At nine years old, Sage already looked like he

belonged onstage at a comedy club. A mess of curly strawberry-blond hair exploded from the top of his head, and two freckled, pudgy cheeks took up most of his face. His red eyebrows hovered over his eyes in a look of permanent confusion.

"Sage, why are you doing that?" said Rose.

"I saw Ty do it with popcorn, and he caught most of it in his mouth."

Ty was their big brother, the oldest Bliss child, and he had one of those faces that made everyone melt. He had wavy red hair and wild gray eyes like a Siberian husky. He was fifteen and played every sport there was to play, and though he wasn't always the tallest, he was always the handsomest. He was exactly the sort of boy who could toss a handful of popcorn in the air and catch all of it in his mouth. The only thing he couldn't do was be bothered to help with the bakery. But their parents didn't seem to mind much. Ty's face was like a get-out-of-jail-free card that worked better and better with each passing year.

Mr. Borzini, who himself was shaped like a peanut, lumbered out from the back storage room. "Hiya, Rosie!" he said with a grin. Then he saw the macadamia nuts on the floor and his grin disappeared. "Hello, Sage."

"We need a pound of poppy seeds," said Rose with a smile.

"P*rrr*onto!" Sage said, rolling the *r* like an Italian and kissing his fingers. Mr. Borzini's frown melted away and he laughed.

Mr. Borzini smiled at Rose as he handed over the seeds. "You sure got a funny brother, Rosie!"

Rose smiled back, wishing that someone thought she was as funny as Sage. She was quietly sarcastic, but that wasn't the same thing. She wasn't gorgeous, like Ty. She was too old to be adorable, like Leigh. She was good at baking, which mostly meant that she was meticulous and good at math. But no one ever smiled at her and said, "Wow! How meticulous and good at math you are, Rose!"

And so Rose had come to think of herself as merely

ordinary, like a person walking silently in the background of a movie set. Oh well.

Rose thanked Mr. Borzini and loaded the burlap sack of seed into the metal basket on the front of her bike. Then she dragged her brother outside, and the two of them took off.

"I don't understand why we have to go get all this stuff," Sage grumbled as they worked their way up a hill. "If Leigh spilled it, then *she* should have to go get it."

"Sage. She's three."

"I don't understand why we have to work in the stupid bakery anyway. If our parents can't run the bakery by themselves, then they shouldn't have started one in the first place."

"You know they have to bake, it's in their blood," Rose replied, taking a breath. "Plus, this town would collapse without them. Everyone needs our cakes and pies and muffins, just to keep going. We are running a public service."

As much as she rolled her eyes, Rose secretly loved

to help. She loved the way her mother sighed with relief whenever Rose returned with all the right ingredients, loved the way her father hugged her after she'd made a shortbread dough just crumbly enough, loved the way the townspeople hummed with happiness after taking the first warm, flaky bite of a chocolate croissant. And she loved how the mixture of ingredients—some normal, some not so normal—not only made people happy, but sometimes did much more than that.

"Well, I want a copy of the Calamity Falls child-labor codes, because I'm pretty sure what they do to us is illegal."

Rose slowed and clamped her nose as Sage rode past. "So is the way you smell."

Sage gasped. "I do *not* smell!" he said, but then lifted his arms in the air to double-check. "Okay, maybe a little bit!"

2. *Florence the Florist. A dozen poppies.*

Rose and Sage found Florence the Florist asleep in a comfy chair in a corner. Everyone speculated about her exact age, but the consensus in Calamity Falls was that she couldn't be younger than ninety.

Her store looked more like a living room than a floral shop—yellow sunlight splashed through the shutters onto a little sofa, and a fat tabby cat lay splayed out near a dusty fireplace. A collection of vases near the window were filled with every conceivable kind of flower, and a dozen baskets hung from the ceiling with leafy green vines spilling out of them.

Rose brushed a curtain of ivy away from her face and cleared her throat.

Florence slowly opened her eyes. "Who is that?"

"It's Rosemary Bliss," Rose said.

"Oh, I see." Florence grumbled as if she were annoyed at the prospect of having a customer. "What . . . can . . . I . . . get for you?" she asked, rising and panting as she shuffled toward the vases below the window.

"A dozen poppies, please," Rose said.

Florence groaned as she bent to collect the papery red flowers. She perked up, though, as she looked over at Sage. "Is that you, Ty? You're looking ... . shorter."

Sage laughed, flattered to be mistaken for his older brother. "Oh no," he said. "I'm *Sage*. Everyone says we look a lot alike."

Florence grumbled for the second time. "I'll sure miss seeing that heartthrob Ty around when he goes off to college."

Everyone always wondered what her dashingly handsome brother would do when he was finally old enough to leave Calamity Falls. As much as he seemed destined to leave, Rose herself seemed destined to stay behind. She wondered whether, if she remained in Calamity Falls, she'd end up like Florence the Florist—with nothing to do but sleep in a chair in the middle of the day, waiting for something strange and exciting to happen, knowing that it never would.

But leaving town would mean leaving the bakery.

And then she would never get to know where her mother stored all those magical blue mason jars. She'd never learn how to mix a bit of northern wind into icing so that it would thaw the frozen heart of a loveless person. She'd never figure out how to fine-tune the reaction among frog's eyes, molten magma, and baking soda—which, her mother had told her, could mend broken bones almost immediately.

"And what about you, Rosemary?" Florence said as she wrapped the poppies in brown paper. "Anything exciting happening? Any boys?"

"I'm too busy babysitting Sage," Rose said a little too forcefully.

It was true that she didn't have any time to go on dates with boys, but even if she did, she probably wouldn't anyway. A date seemed strange and a little unappealing, like sushi. She would like very much to stand with Devin Stetson at the top of Sparrow Hill and look down at the expanse of Calamity Falls, fall wind blowing through their hair, rustling the leaves.

But that wasn't a date.

Still, he was the reason she'd taken a shower before she left this morning, combed the knots out of her shoulder-length black hair, and put on her favorite pair of jeans and a blue shirt with just the right amount of lace (very little). She knew she wasn't ugly, but she wasn't stunning, either. Rose was sure that if there was any greatness in her at all, it lurked somewhere inside of her and not on her face.

Her mother seemed to agree. "You're not like other girls," she'd once said. "You're so good at math!"

As Rose wondered why she couldn't be both—the kind of girl who was good at math *and* pretty—she and Sage left the shop, poppies in hand.

*3. Poplar's Open-Air Market. 2 lbs. pippin apples.*

A short burst of ferocious pedaling carried them over the train tracks to Poplar's Open-Air Market, which was so crowded in the early morning that the lanes between the rows of fruit and vegetable stands were like a parkway during a traffic jam.

"I need apples!" yelled Rose, waving one hand in the air.

"Aisle three!" a man yelled from behind a table stacked higher than his head with peaches.

Sage stopped the flow of traffic by picking up two giant butternut squashes and lifting them like dumbbells.

"Why are you doing that?"

"I'm getting strong—like Ty," he puffed, his face turning beet red. "Ty and I are going to be pro athletes. There's no way I'm going to stay here and bake for the rest of my life."

Rose grabbed the butternut squashes from Sage's outstretched arms and put them back where they belonged. "But we help people," Rose whispered to Sage. "We're like good baker wizards."

"If we're wizards, then where are our wands and our

owls and magic hats? And where is our arch-nemesis?" Sage said. "Face it, Sis—we're just bakers. While you're stuck here making cakes, me and Ty will be modeling sneakers in France."

Sage pedaled off and Rose was left holding the apples, her arms trembling under the weight.

*4. Mr. Kline's Key Shop. You know what to do.*

In a rusty shack on the outskirts of town, Rose handed Mr. Kline the delicate whisk-shaped key. He examined it through glasses as thick as English muffins.

The key shop was windowless, and everything in it was covered in a fine layer of gray dust, as if Mr. Kline had just come back from a very long vacation. Rose breathed in through her mouth. The air tasted like metal.

"This'll take me half an hour," he said. "You may want to come back."

Sage let out a ridiculously loud groan, but Rose was happy. Kline's just happened to sit at the base of Sparrow Hill, and Stetson's just happened to sit at the top.

"Hey, buddy," she said. "Let's walk up Sparrow Hill."

"No way!" Sage said. "That hill is way too high and it's way too hot. I'm gonna see if they have any new jelly bean flavors at Calamity Confections."

"Come on," said Rose, catching him by the shoulder. "It'll be nice. We can stand on the fence at the lookout point and find our house. And I'll buy you a donut."

"Fine. But," he said, raising one finger high above his head, "I get to pick the donut!"

## 5. Stetson's Donuts and Automotive Repair

Rose was panting by the time they reached the top of the hill. Stetson's was an unimpressive concrete hut adorned with the parts of old cars. Pansies grew out of tires on the ground, and a DONUTS sign hung from an old fender fixed above the doorframe.

Rose trembled as she scooped her black hair, now goopy with sweat, away from her forehead. She was the kind of girl who was unafraid of spiders, dirt bikes, or burning her fingers in a hot oven—and she'd had plenty of encounters with each. But walking into the same room as a boy she liked? Now *that* was frightening.

Just as she gathered the courage to walk down the drive and enter the store, Devin Stetson breezed by on his moped, blond bangs flapping in the wind, and sped down the hill. Apparently his father had given him the morning off.

Rose's stomach turned. It was the same sensation as when you fly higher than you should on a swing set and you can feel your stomach a beat behind, flopping around inside you like a fish on the deck of a boat.

As she watched him go, she could swear he turned

for a second and glanced back at her.

Sage had already ambled up to the lookout point and climbed to the second rail of the fence. "Whoa. Rose. Look."

Rose shook herself and jogged over to see what Sage was talking about: A caravan of police cars was driving along the winding road that cut through town. Calamity Falls looked like a painting from the top of Sparrow Hill, and the cars looked like a blue and white knife slashing through it.

"Where are they going?" asked Sage, uncharacteristically quiet.

"Oh boy," Rose said, squinting. "I think they're going to the bakery."

## CHAPTER 2
# A Hammer Falls

"Maybe Ty was arrested," said Rose.

She and Sage threw their bikes down in the Bliss bakery backyard and ran toward the back door. Three police cruisers formed a fence outside the house, and a white Hummer with tinted windows squatted in the driveway like a fat pit bull.

Through the open driver's-side window of the Hummer, Rose and Sage could see a man wearing a crisp police uniform and sunglasses. He was speaking into a walkie-talkie. "They're still in there," he was saying. "I know them—they won't come out empty handed."

Rose stepped on a cinder block and peered through the open shutters of one of the kitchen windows. Her parents were standing on one side of the great wooden chopping block that Purdy rolled around like a shopping cart. A woman in a stern navy pantsuit stood on the other side. Purdy and Albert looked at each other nervously while Purdy kept a hand on the Bliss Cookery Booke, which sat closed on the chopping block. When the book was open, it looked like a fat white bird spreading its wings; closed, it looked vulnerable, like a little loaf of brown bread.

*This is it,* Rose thought. *Someone has come for the book.*

Every Tuesday evening, Albert and Purdy went to two-for-one night at the Calamity Falls Movie Theater and left their neighbor Mrs. Carlson in charge. As

Albert left, he'd always say, "Don't let anyone in! It might be the government coming to steal our recipes!"

The kids always laughed, but Rose knew that her father wasn't really joking. She'd glimpsed pages in the book with medieval drawings of storms, fire, a wall of thorns, a man bleeding—recipes you wouldn't want to fall into the hands of someone who might actually use them.

Sage climbed up on the cinder block but couldn't see through the window. "What's going on?" he asked.

"They're going to take the cookbook," she said, struggling to push the words past a massive lump in her throat. She looked in at the strange cast-iron stove that sat like a dark beehive against one wall of the kitchen, at the row of glistening cherrywood cabinets that lined the other, at the tangle of racks and metal hooks that hung in a cluster from the center of the ceiling and held at their ends every conceivable size of metal spatula and spoon, at the giant silver stand mixer that sat in the back corner, with a bowl so big that Leigh could (and sometimes did) climb inside, and a twirling dough hook the size of a rowboat's oar. She stared at everything her parents had built, shabby as it was, and stifled a sob.

She imagined her parents locked in a dirty jail cell, her brothers begging on the streets, the country ruled by a mob of tyrannical bakers who used muffins and pies as their weapons of mass destruction.

"I'll stop them," Sage muttered, and rushed around to the back door. He threw it open and shouted, "My parents didn't do anything!"

Albert and Purdy spun around inside the kitchen and tried to shush Sage, but it was too late. The woman in the navy pantsuit stared out the backdoor and motioned for Sage and Rose to come inside.

"My name is Janice 'The Hammer' Hammer," she said. "I'm the mayor of Humbleton." She flashed a strained smile, and Rose realized that though this wasn't the friendliest woman she'd ever met, she wasn't there to steal their book, either.

"Why are the police here?" said Rose.

"Those are cars that I had painted to look like police cars so that I'd look more intimidating whenever I went on a trip. The men inside are my colleagues on the Humbleton Board of Trustees. One is a florist, one is a lawyer, and the third is a plumber who fills in when he doesn't have any toilets to unclog."

"Isn't it illegal to dress up like a police officer?" Sage prodded.

Mayor Hammer just glared at him. "I came to ask your parents for help in fighting a summer flu in Humbleton. I've never seen one this bad—it's like a plague. Garbage cans overflowing with Kleenex. Doctors totally out of cough drops. The ear, nose, and throat guy fleeing in terror to his condo in Florida. Wimp."

Albert and Purdy laughed nervously.

"Anyway, I didn't know what to do. But then I remembered your parents' almond croissants—people swear they make fevers and runny noses just disappear.

So I've come to beg for forty dozen."

Mayor Hammer turned back to Albert and Purdy. "I know it's short notice, but I've run out of options."

Purdy wrung her hands. "We—we'd love to help," she stammered, "but this kitchen really doesn't have the capacity to make forty dozen croissants. We're just a family bakery."

"Come to Humbleton, then!" blurted out Mayor Hammer. "You could feed an army out of the kitchen at Town Hall. You'll make your almond croissants there. And then you'll make pumpkin cheesecake."

"Pumpkin cheesecake?" asked Albert, his forehead wrinkling.

Mayor Hammer reached into her black leather briefcase and pulled out a yellowed newspaper clipping from the *Calamity Falls Gazette*. The headline read, "Ten-Year-Old Boy with Swine Flu Eats Bliss Pumpkin Cheesecake, Miraculously Cured."

Albert wiped his hands on his apron. "Ha! Wouldn't that be something? That was just a tall tale, though.

The kid was faking so he could skip school."

Her parents never admitted to anyone but their children that Bliss baked goods had magic in them. "If word gets out about the magic," Purdy always said, "then everyone will want it, and our little bakery won't be our little bakery anymore. It will become a giant factory. Everything would be ruined."

If anyone noticed the sometimes miraculous effects of the cookies, the cakes, the pies, Albert and Purdy would shrug it off, insisting that these were the standard benefits of a perfect recipe, well prepared.

Rose, though, could still remember when that cheesecake had been made. She'd been watching from the stairs, observing how her parents had sifted the ingredients from a few different mason jars together one night after the bakery was closed, how a purple mist had risen from the bowl and swirled around her mother's head, how the mixture had sizzled and popped, shooting off sparks of pink and green and canary yellow.

What she wouldn't give to bake like that! It was a kind of baking that commanded respect, even if the whole thing was kept a secret.

Mayor Hammer tapped her foot impatiently. "I don't care whether the cheesecake actually cures people or not—people love it, it makes them feel better, and that's what we need."

Purdy made her voice soft and sweet as a chocolate chip cookie. "Well . . . how long do you need us?"

"No more than a week," said the mayor.

Albert shook his head. "I'm sorry, Mayor Hammer. We've been open for twenty-five years, and we've never closed the bakery for more than a single day. There's just no way we can leave for an entire week."

Mayor Hammer nodded to one of her bodyguards, who produced a leather-bound checkbook. She scribbled some numbers on a check and showed it to Albert and Purdy, who looked at each other in shock, like someone had just pulled a rabbit out of a hat—a very expensive, diamond-encrusted rabbit.

Albert gasped. "So many zeros."

Purdy looked at Mayor Hammer with embarrassment. "We'll do it—"

"Oh, wonderful!" said Mayor Hammer, handing Purdy the check.

Purdy tore the check into pieces. "You didn't let me finish! We'll do it, *for free.*"

Rose smiled. Her parents could be the richest people in the world—CEOs wearing fancy gray suits, sipping fancy champagne, riding in the back of a fancy car, like Mayor Hammer—but they would rather live in the simple rooms above the cramped kitchen of their tiny bakery.

Mayor Hammer reached across the chopping block and hugged Albert and Purdy to her chest. "We'll take you on over as soon as you're ready," she said. "I'll be waiting in the Hammer Hummer."

Rose banged on the door to Ty and Sage's room. A handwritten sign read VISITING HOURS: 3 P.M. TO 4 P.M.

"Ty!" Rose called. "Mom and Dad are going away! *Please* come downstairs."

It was only eleven in the morning, and Ty rarely emerged from his cave before midafternoon. Rose cracked open the door. Ty had strung up a sheet to divide his and Sage's sections of the room—Ty's was behind the sheet, of course—but just past the edge of the sheet, Rose could make out a single white sock dangling off her older brother's foot.

She pulled the sheet back and poked his broad, bare back. "Ty."

Ty groaned. "You better have an amazing excuse for coming in here," he said, "because you woke me up in the middle of a basketball dream."

"Mom and Dad are leaving for a week. She is putting *us* in charge of the bakery!"

As soon as she said the words out loud, Rose imagined herself dancing around the kitchen in her mother's blue-and-white-checkered apron, leafing through the Bliss Cookery Booke, sifting flour and melting chocolate and mixing in the tears of heartbroken young girls, or a vial of a good man's last breath, or a pat of the chalky, bitter powder made from the ashes of summer campfires, or—who knew what she might use? Then she would turn the crank to raise the secret lightning rod that sometimes powered the main oven, and just like that, she'd be making magic. Rose sometimes grumbled when her parents asked her to help with the bakery, but only because the help never entailed any real magic.

The real magic, the blue-mason-jar magic, she imagined, would be worth all the trouble.

"Are you serious?" said Ty, bolting up. "This is great!"

"I know!" said Rose. "We'll get to actually bake!"

Ty scoffed. "Correction, *mi hermana*." Ty had taken to using Spanish whenever he could, in preparation for the day when he would finally become a pro skater in Barcelona. "*You'll* get to actually bake. *I'll* get to actually relax."

\* \* \*

Downstairs, Albert closed the shutters on all the kitchen windows, while Purdy lit a candle. Rose imagined that this was what it was like to be sworn into a secret society. She stood at attention, awaiting her parents' instructions. Ty was slouched across the rolling chopping block, his chin in his hands, moaning with boredom.

"We don't want to leave you," said Purdy, "but our neighbors need us. We've asked Chip to come in full-time this week, but he can't do all the baking *and* run the counter, so we need you two to pitch in more than usual."

Rose shivered with excitement as Albert picked up the Bliss Cookery Booke.

"First things first," he said, opening the stainless steel door of the walk-in refrigerator and carrying the Booke inside.

Rose and Ty followed their father through a narrow hallway lined floor to ceiling with cartons of ordinary milk, butter, eggs, chocolate chips, pecans, and more. A dim fluorescent bulb flickered from above.

At the end of the hallway hung a faded green tapestry.

Rose had seen it before, when she would unload cartons of eggs after a trip to the poultry farm, and it had always captivated her. It was thick, like a Persian rug, and covered in delicately embroidered pictures: A man kneading dough. A woman stoking a fire in an oven. A child in a nightgown eating a little cake. An old man using a net to capture fireflies. A girl sifting a snowfall onto a frosting.

Purdy rested her hand on Rose's shoulder. "Honey, do you have the key you copied this morning?"

Rose patted her breast pocket and removed the two silver keys—the tarnished one her mother had given her that morning and the shiny new one that Mr. Kline had just made. She handed them to her father, who pocketed the old key, then pulled back the tapestry to reveal a short wooden door with faded planks and cast-iron bars, the kind of door made back when people were shorter. He pushed the delicate prongs of the shiny new whisk-shaped key inside the lock on the door, which looked like an eight-pointed star, and turned to the left.

The door creaked open. Albert yanked an old brass chain, and a dusty bulb came to life overhead.

Rose stood with her mouth agape.

Beyond the door was a tiny wood-paneled room the size of a short closet, crowded with medieval treasures. A painting of a thin, mustached man wearing a long robe the color of an eggplant—on the frame was written HIERONYMUS BLISS, FIRST MAGICK BAKER in old English lettering that was almost impossible to read. An engraving of an aproned woman serving a piping hot pie to a king at a long banquet table: ARTEMISIA BLISS, WOMAN BAKER, HONORED BY CHARLES II. A sepia-toned photograph of a man and woman holding hands outside a bakery, alongside a newspaper clipping from 1847: "Bliss Bakers Arrive on Lower

East Side, Feed Immigrants." The four of them stood, huddled in the storeroom, peering at the ancient artifacts by candlelight. "Your mother and I call this room the library, even though there's only one book in it. The book is more important than all the books in all the libraries in this whole country, combined. So this is a library."

Even Ty was impressed. "Bet you're glad you became a Bliss, huh, Pop?"

Albert nodded. When he married Purdy, Albert had taken her name instead of the other way around. "Who wants to cling to a name like Albert Hogswaddle," he'd said, "when you could become Albert Bliss?"

Albert sat the Bliss Cookery Booke on a dusty pedestal in the middle of the little storeroom, and they all huddled around, barely fitting inside the room. "The book stays here. No one opens it, no one moves it. Rose, I am giving you the key to this room." He slid it onto a string, knotted it, and handed it over. Rose wondered briefly how her mother had known they'd need an extra key. But then she shrugged it away: Her mother just *knew* things. It was part of her magic.

Rose took the key from his outstretched palm and hung it around her neck. She burned with excitement.

"But you are *not* to open this door unless there is a fire," Albert said, the ever-present smile suddenly gone from his face. "In which case you should try to save the book. I repeat: Do not open this door. There will be NO magic."

All the excitement flew out of Rose, and she deflated like a popped balloon. *No magic? Why?*

"Tick tock, people!" shouted Mayor Hammer from inside the Hummer. "The flu is spreading even as we speak!"

Albert huffed and puffed in the background as he hauled six leather suitcases from the house to the driveway and loaded them into the Hummer. One was filled with clothes, the other five loaded down with jars of Madagascar cinnamon and dried fairy wings, with special black sugars from a forest in Croatia and trapped doctors' whispers, with dozens of things mundane and mysterious.

Purdy gathered Rose and her siblings together in one big clump in the driveway. "Rose and Ty, you'll help Chip in the kitchen."

Ty groaned. "Why do I have to help? That's Rose's territory."

Purdy patted Ty sympathetically on his beautiful, tawny cheek. "I know you can do it, Thyme." She went on, looking at Sage. "Sage, you'll stay with your sister Rose. I mean, help her."

"Of course! I will be *very* helpful," Sage said, winking devilishly at Rose and everyone else.

Rose rolled her eyes. Sage's idea of helping usually involved whining and trying to burp the alphabet.

Albert finished loading the suitcases. "Mrs. Carlson will be coming this afternoon and staying all week to watch Leigh. Be nice to her and do as she says."

"But she yells in her Scottish accent and it hurts

my ears!" said Sage. "And she falls asleep all the time while she's tanning or watching TV. And she smells weird."

"That's not being nice, pal," said Albert. "But . . . you're not wrong. Rose, just keep an extra eye on Leigh, in case Mrs. Carlson falls asleep."

Purdy smiled wide, even though two fat tears were rolling down her cheeks. "We love you all!" she said.

"Wait!" Leigh screamed. "Picture!"

Purdy laughed. "All right. Mayor Hammer, would you mind taking a family picture?"

Mayor Hammer sighed loudly in a way that meant that she minded very much, but still, she grabbed the Polaroid camera from Leigh's outstretched hands, pointed it in the direction of the Bliss clan, and clicked the shutter.

Then Purdy and Albert hopped into the backseat and shut the door behind them. The Hummer lumbered down the street, three fake police cars filing after it.

Rose turned to Ty. She wanted to say something

like, "I'm happy we're going to be spending some time together this week." But Ty was already strolling down the driveway toward the street.

"My vacation officially starts"—he said, pushing a button on his watch—*"now!"* So much for Ty spending time in the bakery. Rose sighed. Her brothers never paid any attention to her, not even now.

Sage had already resumed jumping on the trampoline.

Leigh tugged on Rose's shirt. "Rosie Posie! An emergency!" she shrieked.

"What, Leigh?"

"A slug! I stepped on a slug!" Leigh lifted her sneaker to reveal a gooey corpse.

Rose undid the Velcro straps on Leigh's shoes, which used to be white but were now the color of a puddle, and wiped the sole on the grass until the dead slug came loose.

Leigh stared at the creature with her big black eyes. Everyone always said that Leigh looked like a miniature version of Rose—black hair, black bangs, black eyes, tiny nose—only cuter. There was something about the roundness of her little face that Rose's lacked, and not just because she was older.

"Should we have a funeral for him?" Leigh asked.

"The slug?" Rose asked.

Leigh nodded solemnly and thrust the Polaroid picture into Rose's hand: Purdy and Albert smiled widely, their arms wrapped around handsome Ty, hysterical Sage, adorable Leigh. Rose stood off to the side, but you wouldn't know it was Rose, because only her shoulder had made it into the photo.

Rose shoved the picture back at Leigh and began another week of the same old thankless routine.

## CHAPTER 3
# A *Mysterious Stranger*

*T*o Rose, the prospect of helping Chip was far more terrifying than finding a slug.

Chip, who had been Purdy's kitchen helper since before Rose could remember, was already at the bakery, staring through the kitchen window, past the slug and past the swing set and past the hedges, past Calamity Falls. He was bald and tan and looked like he had just walked off a photo shoot for the cover of a bodybuilding magazine.

The one conversation Rose had ever had with Chip involved the silver metal ID tags he wore on a chain around his neck.

"Were you in the army, Chip?" she'd asked.

"The marines," he'd grunted.

"Then why are you working as a helper in a bakery?" she'd asked.

He squatted down so that his face was square with hers. He breathed noisily, staring her in the eye. "I like to bake," he'd whispered.

Rose pictured what the week ahead would be like—having to bake alongside the hulking bulk of Chip's chiseled torso, and having to use the recipes in the boring old Betty Crocker cookbook, which Albert and Purdy had given to Chip before they left.

"Here, Chip—use these recipes."

He'd snorted. "What about your special cookbook?"

"This one is easier to read," Purdy had said, handing him the paperback book with an ordinary cherry pie on the cover.

She was terribly upset that her parents weren't allowing them to use the magical Cookery Booke while they were away.

It wasn't fair. She had devoted her life to the bakery!

It was Rose who woke up early to help her parents prepare for the day while other kids her age were still sleeping. It was Rose who came home straight after school because she was needed to help clean the bakery in the afternoons. And Rose did it all without complaint, in the hope that one day she, too, would become a kitchen magician. And now her parents were denying her the only thing she'd ever wanted: to bake something magical.

And it was Rose who got stuck helping her little sister when no one else wanted the job. Rose looked down at Leigh, who was digging a hole with her hands in which to bury the fallen slug.

"I'm not in the mood for a funeral," said Rose. "I'll push you on the swing. Come on."

Leigh left the slug and bounded over to the swing set, a wooden contraption that Albert had erected a year earlier. The wood was wet and green with mold, and the rusty chains creaked as Rose heaved her little sister back and forth.

"Push!" Leigh pumped at the air as hard as she could by swinging her knobby knees. "Higher, Rosie, higher!"

Leigh was wearing her filthy red-and-white-striped shirt and red-and-white-striped headband, the same ones she insisted on wearing every day. When they were absolutely covered with mud stains and juice spills and marker mishaps, Rose stole them from Leigh's room while she was asleep and popped them in the wash.

*Haven't I earned the right to try a little magic?* thought Rose. *When is all of this errand running and babysitting going to get me anywhere?*

A minute later, Rose heard the faint buzzing of a motorcycle. The sound drew closer and closer to the house. Rose's heart thumped in her chest like an angry bullfrog trapped in a shoe box. She only knew one person in town who rode a motorcycle (or moped, anyway), and his name was Devin Stetson.

Her mind raced to throw together a few things to say if he were to stop in her driveway and stroll into the backyard.

*Hi. How are you? My name is Rose. Have we met? Why are you in my backyard?*

He would say that he saw that caravan of police cars and was worried about her. Then he would say that he needed to get to Poplar's Open-Air Market because his father wanted to start making blueberry donuts, but he didn't know where it was.

*I know where it is*, she'd say. *Let me show you.*

Then she'd climb onto the back of his moped, and her knees would brush against his dark denim jeans. She would rest her chin on his shoulder for the entire ride and feel the sting of his blond hair whipping her cheeks in the wind. Even if they hit a rock and she was tossed into a ditch and broke both legs, it would be worth it.

But Rose wasn't like other girls her age. Rose had responsibilities.

The frantic whirring of the motorcycle slowed a bit as it pulled into the driveway. But this was not Devin Stetson's rusty red moped—this was a gleaming black beast with a head shaped like a bull, with a silver saddle and sharp silver horns for handlebars. A figure sheathed entirely in black leather hopped off the saddle and leaned against the body of the motorcycle.

Rose's heart raced. There had already been too many ominous people in her driveway that day.

She turned to see if Chip was still watching from the kitchen window—Chip would be able to tackle this person, whoever it was, if it came to that—but he was nowhere to be found.

Rose stepped in front of Leigh to guard her.

The figure removed its black helmet with gloved hands coated in silver spikes.

The rider was a young woman—the tallest, most sensational-looking woman Rose had ever seen outside

54

of a movie screen. She had strong black eyebrows, a long Roman nose, and short black hair cropped close to her scalp in a chic pixie cut. Her full lips were painted red, and her big white teeth glinted in the sun. She was the kind of woman who looked like she belonged in the pages of a magazine—the kind of woman Rose secretly wished she would grow up to become.

"Ahhhhh!!!" the woman exclaimed. "Fresh air! A small town! I *love* a small town!" She tossed a throaty laugh to the sky, then undid the metal clasps on her black leather jacket and tossed it onto the bike. She was wearing a lacy blue shirt underneath, much like the one Rose was wearing.

"You must be Rosemary!" she said, sauntering toward the swing set. She indicated her shirt. "Look at us! We're twins!"

When the woman in the black leather got close enough, Leigh bolted into the kitchen, leaving Rose clutching the rusty metal chains of the swing.

"Don't look so frightened, pet! I'm your aunt Lily!"

This woman, whoever she was, was smiling ear to ear with all of her gleaming, fancy white teeth. Could Rose really be related to someone so . . . beautiful? She looked more like a fashion model than an aunt.

Rose conjured up a mental image of the Bliss family tree she'd made for an assignment on genealogy back in the third grade—it was a short, very wide piece of white poster board on which she'd drawn her and her siblings' names: Parsley, Sage, Rosemary, Thyme; and above that, her parents' names: Albert Hogswaddle, Purdy Bliss. Her aunts and uncles: on her father's side were Aunt Alice, Aunt Janine, and weird Uncle Lewis. On her mother's side: no one. There was no Lily. The name did ring a bell, but Rose couldn't remember why.

"Is your mother here?" she asked. "Oh, I hope I came at a good time! I miss old Purdy Bliss!"

Rose spoke cautiously. "My mother never told me she had a younger sister."

Lily laughed again, her long neck arched back. "She doesn't!"

Rose must have looked confused. "I'm not your *aunt*, per se," Lily said. "Your mother's great-great-great-grandfather Filbert Bliss had a brother named Albatross, and that was my great-great-great-grand-father, so I believe that makes us . . . fifth cousins once removed! But *Aunt Lily* has such a nice ring to it, don't you think?"

Rose pictured the family tree in her mind's eye, trying to remember if there were any Albatrosses or Filberts, but the tree morphed into a twisted, over-grown thicket.

"Anyway, I heard my dear Purdy had a baby! And started a bakery!"

"Four babies," said Rose, shielding her eyes from the sun with her hand.

"Well! Seems I'm a little late!"

Lily sauntered back to the motorcycle and began removing her gloves, finger by finger. "You see, *I* am a baker as well! I've published a cookbook—well, I pub-lished it myself. But it's the same difference! I even had my own radio show for a few months, *Lily's Ladle*! Surely you heard about it!"

Rose had never heard of a radio show called *Lily's Ladle*, but she suddenly remembered where she'd heard the name *Lily*. It was several years ago. One night after dinner, Rose was helping her father clear the dishes while Purdy took a phone call. It was the kind of phone call where her mother didn't do much talking, but just leaned against the kitchen counter, speechless, wrapping the cord around her finger, then unwrapping.

When she hung up, Rose and Albert stared at her, waiting.

"It was *Lily*," she said. Albert's eyes went wide. "She found us. She wants to come for a *visit*."

Albert winced. "You said no, right?"

"Of course," said Purdy.

"Who is Lily?" asked Rose.

"No one," said Purdy, heading upstairs.

Rose snapped out of her memory, then walked up to Lily and tapped her on the shoulder. "Come to think of it, I have heard of you. My mother talked to you on the phone a while back. She didn't want you to come for a visit," Rose said, her heart beating thunderously. "Why didn't she want you to come for a visit?"

Lily raised her eyebrows. "A long time ago, my great-great-great-grandfather Albatross had a terrible fight with your great-great-great-grandfather Filbert, and now Purdy won't speak to me, and it's such a shame. So I've come here to mend old fences!"

"You mean . . . old bridges?" said Rose.

"Exactly!" Lily smiled. "Look, darling, I know you don't believe me, but I am your cousin! Or your aunt! Same difference! I have the family mark to prove it!"

Lily turned around and pulled down one side of the back of her blue shirt, revealing her shoulder blade, which was as elegant as an angel's wing. Rose squinted and saw a strange birthmark, a blob with a long handle of dark trailing off it, the end hooked.

Rose had one just like it on the side of her leg. Leigh had one on her neck. Purdy had one on her arm.

Ty and Sage both had one on their stomachs. They all had one.

"See, darling?"

Sage ran out from the kitchen to investigate the black bull that had landed in the driveway. He saw the mark on Lily's back and shouted, "You've got the ladle!"

Lily spun around and tried to hoist Sage's hefty torso up in her arms, then thought the better of it and set him down. "You must be Sage!"

Sage giggled and squirmed. "Who *are* you?"

Lily pressed a finger to his nose and rubbed it back and forth. "I'm your aunt Lily!" she said, and curtsied with a flourish. "And I've come to rejoin my family!"

## CHAPTER 4

# Aunt Lily Helps Out

"My mother isn't here," Rose said, fidgeting with the hem of her shirt.

Aunt Lily walked over to her motorcycle and unhooked a small tweed suitcase and a smaller bag in the shape of a log, made of crushed crimson velvet that changed color depending on the way you looked at it.

"Looks like I arrived at just the right time, Rose!" said Lily. "What better way to show your parents I want to heal our troubled relationship than to help their children out when they're away?"

Rose thought that the whole thing sounded fishy, at best. She prayed that her parents would suddenly waltz back into the driveway and announce that they'd forgotten their underwear.

But there was no waltzing.

"Maybe you should come back when my parents are here."

Lily made a face like a wounded dog. "I just thought I could help. With the bakery." She picked up her suitcase and bag and gingerly hooked them onto the back of her motorcycle. "But I can see that you'd like me to go."

"Noooooooo!" Sage yelled. "Rose, what are you doing? You can't send a family member away! I mean, she has the ladle!"

Rose looked at the glamorous professional baker who was offering to help her for a week. Then she looked at Sage, her only sous-chef, who chose that moment to pick his nose. There would be too much work that week for her and Chip to do by themselves, and she had a feeling that Ty and Sage and Leigh were not going to step up to the plate. Besides, there was something about this woman that made Rose unable to look away from her—even if she was fishy, at best.

"Wait!" Rose called to Lily. "I guess . . . we really could use the help."

"Wheeeee!" cried Lily. "I know exactly what we'll make for dinner tonight!"

*What* we'll *make for dinner tonight.*

Rose couldn't help but happily notice: Aunt Lily had said *we.*

Mrs. Carlson shuffled into the backyard later that afternoon. She had her short blond hair in curlers and wore a sequined top and white leggings that were too tight. In one hand she carried a portable TV, and in the other hand she carried a box of porridge and a thing in a clear plastic bag that looked like a stomach and smelled like worse.

Sage pinched the end of his nose. "What is that?"

"I'm going to make haggis," Mrs. Carlson said in her thick Scottish brogue. "Haggis is porridge boiled in the stomach of a sheep. It'll put hair on your chest."

Sage clutched at his chest.

"That's very kind of you, Mrs. Carlson, but it won't be necessary," Rose said nervously.

Mrs. Carlson tilted her head sideways to look at Rose. "Why?"

"Well," Rose began, "our aunt has come for a visit, and she's already started making dinner."

Mrs. Carlson grunted. "Your father didn't say anything about an aunt!"

Rose looked around nervously. "He . . . forgot she was coming. But she's here now. And she'll do all the cooking this week."

Mrs. Carlson shuffled over to the metal garbage

can by the back door and dumped the sheep's stomach inside. "Good. I didn't really want haggis anyway."

Since the entire first floor of the Bliss house was the bakery, the family spent most of their time in the evening crammed around the table in the kitchen. It wasn't so much a table as a booth, like one you'd find at a diner—two high-backed benches of dark wood with red leather cushions facing each other, separated by a varnished cherrywood table, and a medieval-looking cast-iron chandelier above. The family ate breakfast, lunch, and dinner in the booth and often gathered after dinner to resume a never-ending game of crazy eights, trying their best not to elbow one another as they picked cards up and slammed others down.

The boys banged the ends of their forks and knives on top of the table and shouted, "Li-ly! Li-ly!" as they waited for dinner. Leigh perched on top of the table like a frog, her knobby knees flanking her ears. Mrs. Carlson sat squished between Ty and Sage, clutching her leather purse to her chest. "A family of animals!" Mrs. Carlson exclaimed.

Rose shrugged, feeling invisible compared to her louder-than-life siblings.

Aunt Lily had been puttering around in the background of the kitchen for the last hour. She had changed out of her black leather motorcycle outfit and into a flowing white cotton dress, which made her look impossibly tall and clean and elegant, even as she worked in the hot, cramped kitchen. After a while, she set a giant orange serving platter in the center of the table.

"*Paella valenciana!*" she shouted. "This is a rice dish from Spain. I learned to make it while I was studying classical guitar outside Barcelona."

It was a pile of fragrant rice stained the delicate orange color of saffron, with pieces of chicken, spicy red sausage, and a slew of edible sea creatures.

"This looks *delicioso*, *Tía* Lily!" Ty exclaimed, even though he normally refused to eat anything other than buttered noodles and licorice. Tonight he was wearing a crisp button-down and had spiked his hair with gel. Rose guessed it had something to do with the gorgeous woman puttering around the kitchen.

"I just think seafood is so much fun!" Lily said. "My father used to bring mussels and shrimps and clams home all the time. He was a fisherman."

"So your side of the family aren't bakers?" Rose asked, thinking that maybe the birthmark on Lily's shoulder might actually be a fishhook instead of a ladle.

"They tried to be," Lily began, "but they didn't have the right . . . stuff. So they all moved to Nova Scotia and became fishermen instead. But I didn't want that kind of life. So I bought a motorcycle and ran away to New York City to be a glamorous actress!"

"I went there once," croaked Mrs. Carlson through a big gulp of orange rice. "Someone stole my purse, and then a pigeon dropped a you-know-what on my head."

The Bliss kids burst into laughter.

"Sounds like New York City to me!" said Lily, fanning herself. "When I arrived, I soared down Broadway on Trixie—that's my motorcycle—and I felt so desperately, magnificently *alive*! Then I realized I had nowhere to live, and only enough money for a few hot dogs! So I bought myself a few hot dogs, and I ate them in Central Park."

"That's exactly what I would have done, *Tía* Lily," said Ty in his deepest voice. Rose had never seen her brother try so hard to be friendly. And now he was calling this strange woman *Tía* Lily like he'd known her all his life.

"Yes!" Lily cried. "Sometimes one must have a hot dog! In any case, I was wandering west on Seventieth Street, and it was getting dark. I looked over and I saw a little cupcake shop with white shutters and adorable yellow curtains, and a sign in the window saying they needed an assistant. So I marched right in there and I said, 'I will assist you for free if you will let me sleep in the kitchen.' And they did! And that is where I learned to bake."

"Can you take me with you when you go back?" said Sage.

Leigh stood up and began bouncing up and down on the table. "New York City! New York City!"

"Maybe I will take you to New York one day," Lily said, placing a hand softly on Leigh's back to still her while Mrs. Carlson just sat there grimacing. "But I won't be going back for a while. I'm going to host my own TV show, you see. It will be called *30-Minute Magic*. So I am traveling around looking for the best recipes in the country, recipes that are wonderful enough to share with the world."

"Rose!" Sage exclaimed. "Let's show her the book!"

Rose stiffened. "What book?" If Lily was hoping to learn magical recipes, she had come to the wrong place. "Oh, you mean the *books*! The accounting books. Sage thinks you might be interested in our business model."

Lily smiled and shrugged. "Oh, that's okay! I'm a

cook, not a mathematician!"

Rose glared at her little brother, who just stuck out his tongue in return.

The next morning, Rose arrived downstairs to find Ty mopping the front room of the bakery, wearing crisp black slacks and a black shirt and vest. He looked like a waiter.

"You're up!" Rose exclaimed. "And you're—what's wrong with you?"

Ty looked around nervously. "Nothing. I'm cleaning up."

"Since when do you even know how to use a mop?"

"I'm just trying to help the new lady of the house," he said.

Rose wondered if she should have tried harder to look slick that morning. Unlike most of the girls at school, who wore brand-name jeans and fancy jackets with rhinestones on them and expensive-looking tops in bright colors, Rose never much cared about what she wore. For one thing, anything on her body eventually got dirty—with butter or grease or flour or whatever other ingredients were lurking in the Bliss kitchen. And anyway, a new blouse wouldn't make her look like a movie star. It wouldn't make Devin Stetson notice her. It would just make her look like she was trying too hard.

But standing next to Aunt Lily, with all her fabulous clothes, Rose felt like a dirty street urchin and wondered if she shouldn't run out to a store and buy herself something bedazzled.

Rose pushed through the saloon doors that separated the front room from the kitchen and found Chip standing in the corner of the kitchen, beating egg whites in the stand mixer. "The marines!" said Lily, fanning her fingertips in front of her mouth. She was standing at the counter kneading some dough, and had exchanged her black leather for a red sundress with white polka dots. "You know, I was a pastry chef on a cruise ship for a year!"

Chip looked up from the mixer and strode toward Rose. "Morning, Rosie!"

Lily touched his shoulder. "Chip, darling, Rose and I need some girl time. Go have a cup of coffee and relax!"

Chip sighed deeply and happily, then skipped out.

Rose stood with her mouth agape. What exactly had this Aunt Lily done to smooth the gruff crankiness of Chip? Why was her older brother *cleaning*? There was something electric about Aunt Lily, something that made you want to dress your best and wear a smile, but Rose couldn't put her finger on it.

"Help me with these?" Lily asked, removing the bowl of whipped egg whites from the stand mixer and offering Rose a spoon.

The two of them plopped heaping spoonfuls of egg white onto a lined baking sheet. Lily worked quickly but effortlessly, like a twirling ballerina. Her face was a picture of easy concentration: lips pressed together, brow slightly furrowed.

"So, Rose. What is it you'd like to do with your life?" asked Lily.

Rose stared at the ceiling. No one had ever asked her that before. Sometimes all she wanted to do was bake, and sometimes she thought she'd scream if she ever saw a muffin again. Sometimes all she wanted to do was run away from Calamity Falls, and sometimes she thought that if she ever left, her heart would shrivel into a black nut inside her and stop beating altogether.

"I'm not sure," she answered finally.

Lily set the tray of meringues in the oven. "I want to go everywhere and meet everyone in the world. I just don't see how a person can do the same thing day after day, go to the same places, see the same people. I would just *die*."

Rose bristled. Aunt Lily had just summed up her entire existence.

"Well, there's something comforting about doing the same things and seeing the same people," Rose said, peering over the saloon doors into the front room. Ty was just changing the front sign from CLOSED to OPEN, and there was already a line around the block. "See those people? I know all of them."

"Tell me about them," said Lily gently.

"Okay, see the man in the frog sweatshirt, standing at the counter? The first one in line?" Lily nodded. "That's Mr. Bastable, the cabinetmaker." Mr. Bastable had stringy white hair and a black moustache, and had always looked to Rose like a cousin of Albert Einstein. He wore a sweatshirt with a dozen frogs printed on the front. "He gets a carrot-bran muffin every morning."

Lily peered out the door. "What about the little woman behind him with the pointy hair?" The woman was so short, Rose knew, that Lily could only see her hair, which was a grayish tower that came to two peaks on either side of her head, like the ears of a wolf.

"That's Miss Thistle, my biology teacher. She is in love with Mr. Bastable. And I think he is in love with her, too. But they never speak."

Lily gasped. "A secret love! How do you know?"

"One day, Mr. Bastable came to our biology class to show us a slide show of his frogs, and Miss Thistle stared at him the whole time with this very peaceful smile on her face, and he kept looking away from her, but you could tell it was because he didn't want her to see how he felt." Rose was well acquainted with this technique—she used it every time Devin Stetson walked past her in the hallways.

Lily looked at Rose with a shiny wetness in her eyes. "I have a secret." She leaned forward. "I'm not really from Nova Scotia. My father was in the army. We moved to a different place every year. I'm not really from anywhere. So I don't understand what it's like to live in one town your entire life." Lily shook her head and squeezed her eyes closed. When she opened them again, her bright smile had returned. "It just seems so boring! Like everyone here is stuck in their ways and can never change."

Rose stiffened. "Are you talking about my mother, too?"

Lily put her arm around Rose. "I don't mean it in a *bad* way," she said. "It's just . . . your mother made a choice. She had gifts. She could have been famous. But instead she ended up here." Lily smiled widely. "You have gifts too, Rose. I can see it. It's just a matter of what you choose to do with them."

Rose blushed. No one had ever called her gifted before. No one had ever called her anything but Rose.

She was beginning to understand the bizarre spell that had fallen on Ty and Chip. There was a grandeur and a magnificence about this woman that rivaled even unicorns. Either that, or Aunt Lily just always knew the right thing to say.

Ty called back from the kitchen. "*Tía* Lily! More croissants!"

Lily picked up the Betty Crocker cookbook with the ordinary cherry pie on the cover. "Is this your usual recipe book? I'd have thought your mom would have been cooking from something more . . . special."

"Nope, this is it," Rose said nervously. "Ordinary recipes. My mom just adds love."

Time flew smoothly by with Lily at the helm: Leigh bounded through the kitchen as usual, but instead of tripping over her and spilling all the ingredients, as Purdy had, Lily gracefully danced around Leigh and even got her to sit and concentrate: "I need you to count out groups of ten raisins, Leigh, into each muffin tin. Can you do it?"

Leigh nodded her head and sat on the floor, slowly and deliberately plopping raisin by raisin into the muffin tins until she couldn't think anymore, then curled up in a ball and fell asleep by the refrigerator.

Ty smiled at all the ladies from town at the front counter, who oohed and aahed at how handsome he was in his shirt and vest. Chip ferried back and forth between the kitchen and the front room like a waiter at a five-star restaurant, standing as tall as he could and nesting one hand in the small of his back as the other held trays of cookies and cakes high above his head. He looked so mournful when five o'clock rolled around and his shift ended that Lily invited him to stay for dinner.

At dinnertime, Mrs. Carlson was dismayed to find the family sitting Indian style on a quilt in the back-yard, Chip and Lily carving a leg of lamb the size of an air conditioner.

"So. What strange thing will we eat for dinner tonight? Curry?" she spat.

"No, ma'am!" Sage cooed. "This is a leg of lamb with that zeekee!"

*"Tzatziki,"* Lily corrected, laughing. "It's a Greek yogurt sauce."

Leigh sat on Chip's lap and gnawed on the same piece of lamb for a long time, Sage and Ty wiped the juicy yogurt sauce from their mouths with their sleeves, and Mrs. Carlson could barely contain a smile as she sucked down pieces of lamb, which were tender as butter. All the while, Rose stared in disbelief at her aunt, who in less than two days had transformed the knit brows of the Bliss clan into easy smiles.

Leigh lifted the Polaroid camera that was permanently strapped to her neck and snapped a picture of Aunt Lily.

After everyone had finished their lamb, Lily snuck off into the kitchen and reappeared carrying a shallow tart with a pale crumb crust, filled with yellow custard. "I made you all something wonderful for dessert!"

Rose's face fell. She hated lemon tarts.

So did Sage. "Ech! Lemon!" he winced, puckering his mouth like a fish.

"No, no!" Lily cried. "There's no lemon! I absolutely *detest* lemon tarts! No, I guarantee that this is unlike anything you've tried before!" she said, doling out slivers with a long knife. "This is a recipe from my great-great-great-grandfather Albatross."

Rose looked at the slice on her plate. Only the top layer was yellow custard—beneath it were layers of swirling crimson and blue and even something that shimmered like the skin of a fish. When she bit into it, she tasted thick, buttery goop that was sweet and a little salty and, indeed, unlike anything she'd ever had.

The Bliss bunch sat in silence, nibbling on tiny bites of the sublime tart, trying to make it last all night.

"See, this is the sort of special recipe I've been traveling around trying to collect," Lily explained. "Truly unique recipes."

The phone rang from inside the kitchen, but everyone was too engrossed in the tart to notice—even Mrs. Carlson, who sat quietly nibbling, a look of rapture on her face.

Only Leigh, who lost interest in the tart after one nibble, ran into the kitchen and stood on one of the red leather cushions in the booth to answer the old black rotary phone. She called from inside, "Mama is on the phone. Ty, talk to Mama!" She left the receiver dangling from the wall in the kitchen and ran outside to rejoin the group on the picnic blanket.

Ty grumbled and stood up.

Lily grabbed his wrist. "Finish that last bite, Ty—I don't want any to go to waste!"

Ty grinned at the look of Aunt Lily's long, elegant fingers wrapped around his wrist, and, like an obedient dog, popped the remaining chunk of the tart in his mouth and swallowed in one gulp, then paced to the back door, as if in a trance. He found the phone swinging on the cord and listlessly pressed it to his ear.

Rose could hear him speak in the way he always spoke on the phone—mechanical, almost robotic. "Hi . . . Good . . . No, nothing new has happened."

Which wasn't true at all! Aunt Lily had arrived, which was possibly the newest thing that had ever happened in the entire dull history of Calamity Falls.

Rose had the urge to run to the phone and tell her parents all about Aunt Lily, to make sure that she'd done the right thing by letting her into the family business. She told herself she was going to do so, right after this next bite of tart. And then the next bite. And, really, right after she finished cleaning her plate. She just couldn't stop nibbling on the tart. Not even after Ty hung up and sat down in the backyard again, saying, "Oh, it was just the usual—clean up and go to bed early and blah blah blah."

Aunt Lily silenced him by raising a forkful of tart toward his mouth. And then they all quieted and ate in silence until every plate and utensil was licked clean and every crumb of the tart was gone, as if it had never been there in the first place.

Every night before bed, the four Bliss children gathered upstairs in the little bathroom with the green floral wallpaper for a sacred ritual they called Brush Time. The foursome huddled around the tiny white porcelain sink in their flannel pajamas and brushed their teeth together.

Ty stumbled around the bathroom in his one pair of blue lacrosse shorts, shirtless, listlessly dragging the bristles over his tongue. Leigh sort of smeared her mouth with toothpaste and then spat. Only Rose brushed her teeth as they were supposed to do: from the gumline to the tips, twice around, inside and out.

Sage sat on the little rocking chair next to the claw-foot tub with his arms folded across his chest, pouting.

"What's wrong now, Sage?" grumbled Rose as she helped Leigh wipe toothpaste from her lips, nose, and face. But she already knew: He, like the rest of them, was thinking about their "aunt" Lily, who even now was settling into the guest room in the basement.

"Why can't we show Lily the book? She needs recipes for her show! Then when she gets famous, we can visit her and be famous too!"

Ty spat into the sink with gusto. "I'm with Little Bro on this one. She needs our help. I think she would love . . . us if we gave it to her."

Lily's words rang in Rose's brain: *You have gifts too, Rose. . . . It's just a matter of what you choose to do with them.* She looked down at the whisk-shaped key that hung around her neck. "We can't do it. I promised."

"Fine!" shouted Sage. "So just 'cause you're afraid

of Mom and Dad and have to do everything they say, Aunt Lily suffers? Good, kind, wonderful Aunt Lily? Who made us *paella* and helped out in the bakery all day and made us a special dessert that was better than anything Mom and Dad ever made from that stupid cookbook?"

"But we don't even know her!" Rose cried. Why was her desire to do the correct and responsible thing always met with frowns from her brothers?

Then Rose thought of something—what if she could help Lily and herself in one fell swoop? What if, instead of showing Lily the book, Rose could copy some of the recipes and practice them right under Lily's nose? Then, if they still trusted Aunt Lily at the end of the week, they could show her the recipes. That way Rose herself would get to learn a little magic and maybe show her brothers that she wasn't all rules and business. Then maybe she'd tell her mother about it, years later, over a cup of tea, and her mother would laugh and say, *Oh, Rose, what a take-charge kind of person you are! I think you and I should run the bakery together.*

Rose beamed at the thought. "I *guess* it would be all right," she began, "to just copy a few of the recipes out of the book and learn them ourselves; then we can teach them to her at the end of the week. That way she'll just think it's a regular recipe with a few weird ingredients. But she can't know about the book!"

Sage and Ty nodded, smiling. "Lily's gonna love *this*," Ty said.

"Okay," Rose said, putting her toothbrush away, and then Leigh's. "Let's meet in the back of the fridge tomorrow morning before she wakes up and copy some recipes."

The brothers Bliss gave each other a high five, then patted Rose on the back. And for the first time in a while, she felt like they had all come from the same parents.

"For the record: I have a bad feeling about this," Rose said, but Ty and Sage were too busy doing a victory dance to hear. She picked Leigh up in her arms like a baby and plopped her onto her bed. Rose pulled the soft red jersey sheets up to her little sister's chin and tucked them under. "Do you think I'm making a mistake, Leigh?"

But Leigh was already asleep.

## CHAPTER 5
# *The Cookery Booke*

Very early the next morning, Rose tiptoed down the stairs and into the kitchen, still in her nightgown. She had a tiny bad feeling about this whole plan, but a huge thrilled feeling about using the cookbook and being part of a team with her brothers, so that won out.

The sky outside was a pale gray, and little rivers of rain inched their way down the windows, blurring the lines of the backyard. Rose could barely make out the dark form of Aunt Lily's motorcycle sitting in the driveway. Leigh was still asleep in her bed, and as Rose crept down the stairs, she had been able to hear Mrs. Carlson snoring mightily. All was quiet from the basement, so it seemed that Lily was asleep as well.

Ty was crammed into the booth, still wearing his blue lacrosse shorts, a white tank top, and a lime-green walkie-talkie headset that he'd gotten for his birthday a few years before.

"Welcome, Rosemary," he said, motioning for her to sit. "You're right on schedule." He pressed a button on the headset and spoke into the microphone. "Cilantro, come in. Come in, Cilantro."

Rose heard Sage's voice pumped through Ty's earpiece. "Cilantro to Bay Leaf, I'm here. Over."

Rose rolled her eyes. "Your code names are just different herbs?"

"Yeah!" he cried, excited. "Bay Leaf to Cilantro, Bay Leaf to Cilantro. Rosemary flying in. Report to the central hub for duty, Cilantro."

"Why don't I get a code name?" Rose asked.

"You're already an herb. What do you think *Rosemary* means?" Ty said.

"Good point, *Thyme*," Rose said.

Sage slid in his tube socks through the saloon doors from the front room onto the terra-cotta tiles of the kitchen floor wearing flannel pajama pants, a black suit jacket, and black sunglasses. Rose thought her brothers looked like spies at a slumber party, and she giggled as Ty handed her a green headset. Sage peered around dramatically and tiptoed over to the booth.

"Here's the plan," Ty began. He was momentarily distracted by his reflection in the kitchen window and fixed his hair. Then he continued: "We get in, we copy some recipes, we get out. Simple, clean, no collateral damage. I will read out loud, and Rose will copy down what I'm saying, because she has good handwriting—"

"What about me?" asked Sage.

Rose and Ty glanced at each other. "You will look

over my shoulder and make sure I'm pronouncing everything correctly," Ty offered. Sage nodded, happy to be given a key role.

Rose opened the door of the walk-in refrigerator, and the three spies moved through the dark hallway. Rose could see her breath condensing like frost in the cold air. But then the lightbulb overhead flickered and went dead, leaving them in the dark, unable to tell the eggs from the cheese, one wall from the other.

"This is creepy," whispered Sage.

Rose felt for the edge of the scratchy green tapestry at the end of the hallway and pulled it back, then ran her hand over the rough wood and iron of the little door until she felt the keyhole. She felt slightly queasy as she turned the delicate prongs of the whisk-shaped key and opened the library.

Purdy had never let her actually *see* the contents of the recipes in the Bliss Cookery Booke, but now Rose felt that she was entitled, after all the errands and the babysitting, to learn the ancient secrets that were her family inheritance.

"We have to pick ones that are exciting and actually make things happen," said Sage, running his finger along the leather of the cover, which was embossed in an intricate filigree pattern that gave it the look of an ancient cathedral door.

Ty shooed Sage away from the book and opened the cover himself.

Rose peered over his shoulder. "Wait!" she said. "There's the one for the poppy muffins that Mom was making the other morning. Read that one."

On one side of the page was a picture of a shadowy wooden kitchen. An older woman wearing a bonnet and apron was pulling a tray of puffy muffins from an oven, while a man in a wide-brimmed hat and ornate fur coat cried and beat the ground with his fists.

On the other side was the recipe.

But it wasn't like a regular recipe, with a list of ingredients and step-by-step instructions—it was more like a story.

Ty read the introduction aloud:

### *Cakes of Red Poppy,*
### *for the Remembrance of Things Lost.*

*It was in 1518, on the Scottish Isle of Froth, that Lady Gresnil Bliss, wearing a red aprone, did cause the forgetful Lord Fallon O'Lechnod to recall the position of his prized cape. Lord Fallon did say, 'It were jeweled with rubies and lined with ferret! Missing two weeks at least. It were stolen by my rivals.' Lady Bliss did bake him these cakes, and Lord Fallon recall'd that he placed the cape at the dining chair of Priest Pierrod two weekes prior and left without collecting it.*

"What the heck does any of that mean?" Sage asked.

Ty turned to Sage. "I think it means that our great-great-grand-whatever helped a rich guy remember that he forgot his coat at a dinner party." Ty read on while Rose furiously scribbled in her marble notebook:

Gresnil Bliss did place two fists of flour pure as snow in the center of the wooden bowl. She cracked one of the chicken's eggs into the flour, then punctured the golden yolk with the tiniest finger of her LEFT hand while whispering "Oublietto Desoletto" thrice in succession.

Then she did stir an acorn of the black seedes into one fist of the cow's milk while whispering "Souviendo Reviendo." She did pour the milk over the flour and stir the iron spoon five times in the way of the clock's hands. She did sprinkle elephant saliva over the micksture and then blow. She did place one petal of the red poppy in the center of each cake.

It went on like that for a while.

There was a wind from the north. She did rest the cake in the oven HOT as seven flames for the TIME of six songs and then fed it to Lord Fallon O'Lechnod, whose eyes did flash green, and he did recover his cape at the home of Priest Pierrod.

"I didn't know the recipes were . . . like that," Rose said. She looked down at her notes. *An acorn of black seeds? As hot as seven flames? For the time of six songs?* "I have no idea what any of those measurements mean."

Rose stared at her brothers with silent desperation.

Ty checked his watch. "It's seven a.m. Chip will be here soon. We need to hurry. Let's just get these copied down, and we'll figure it out later."

A half hour later, Rose, Sage, and Thyme left the secret storeroom with a word-for-word copy of five recipes to experiment with throughout the week.

When they emerged from the refrigerator, they saw

a shimmering purple figure through the blurry window above the nook, moving around the driveway.

"Who is that?" whispered Rose. They cracked opened the backdoor and peeked out.

It was Aunt Lily, clad in a pair of purple sequined pants and a purple tank top. She was tightening a bolt on her motorcycle with a little silver wrench, her short black hair glistening in the rain. "What is she doing up so early?" Rose whispered.

But instead of answering, her brothers bolted out to greet Aunt Lily. Rose stood in the doorway, not wanting to get her nightgown wet. How come her brothers had never bolted to greet *her*?

Lily dropped the wrench and threw her arms around Ty and Sage. "Men!" she said. "What are you doing up so early! And why are you wearing walkie-talkies?"

Sage and Ty glanced at each other. Sage smiled, but Ty slid his walkie-talkie headset off. "Just playing with Sage," Ty said. "You know. Kid stuff."

"Aha!" Lily said. She noticed Rose standing in the

doorway, listening. "Rose! Good morning!"

"What are *you* doing up, Aunt Lily?" Rose asked.

Lily smiled so big that her gums showed. "I can never sleep past seven—so I thought I'd make the morning ingredient run a little easier by taking one of you on Trixie!" She patted the silver horns of her bull-shaped bike. "Who wants to come? Hills are much easier on a motorcycle!"

Sage raised his hand and jumped up and down. "Me, me, me, me, me, me, me!"

Ty stayed cool as a cucumber, even though Rose knew he was dying to go.

Lily handed Sage a black helmet. Sage jumped two feet in the air, strapped the helmet beneath his chin, and hopped onto the back of the bike. "You'll be next," Lily said, winking at Ty.

"Yeah, definitely. Cool," Ty said, then sauntered back toward the kitchen. "'Scuse me, *mi hermana*," he said. Rose wouldn't budge from the door frame. "What's your problem, Sis?"

She leaned in and looked her older brother right in his brilliant gray eyes. "Something bugs me about Aunt Lily. Why would she get up that early just to work on her motorcycle in the rain? And why did she come to settle a family feud from two hundred years ago during the one week ever that our parents happen to be out of town?"

Ty pushed Rose's arm out of the way. "You're imagining things, Rose. You're just jealous that you don't have a motorcycle, and that you're not six feet tall and gorgeous." Rose was still too young to be gorgeous, but the words stung anyway: She already knew that she didn't really possess the makings of future gorgeousness. She certainly didn't need Ty to remind her.

"I'm going to change into something more presentable," Ty announced as he shuffled up the stairs.

Rose sighed. *I probably am just jealous*, she thought—jealous of Aunt Lily's magnificent laugh and magnificent clothes and magnificent life.

She dragged her feet through the dark of the

walk-in refrigerator once more and pulled back the tapestry. She jiggled the handle of the library door again, just to make sure it was locked.

Then, as she was closing the door of the walk-in, she saw a small dot shimmering on the floor. She bent down to get a closer look.

It was a purple sequin, the kind that were sewn all over Aunt Lily's pants.

Lily had been in the refrigerator that morning.

## CHAPTER 6
# *Recipe the First: Love Muffins*

An hour later, Rose threw open the door to Ty and Sage's room, sending the VISITING HOURS sign cascading from the door. Ty was just pulling back the white sheet that divided the room.

"Can't you read? Does it look like three p.m. to you?" He dug through a pile of socks and T-shirts and pulled out a pair of wrinkled khakis.

"Not now, Ty!" Rose cried. "Look what I just found

in the fridge!" She held the purple sequin on the tip of her finger like a ladybug and shoved it under Ty's nose.

"So?" he yawned.

"*So*, Aunt Lily was *eavesdropping*. While we were copying the recipes! I told you there was something fishy about her!"

Ty scoffed. "Did it ever occur to you, *mi hermana*, that she just wanted milk for her coffee, and that we happen to keep our milk in our refrigerator, like every other family in this country?" He laid the khakis over his bedspread and tried to smooth out the creases with his palm.

"Coffee?" Rose repeated quietly. "Was she drinking coffee?"

"Totally," Ty said. He stood up. "Look, she even left the mug in the drive."

Rose peered out the little white portal at the head of Ty's bed and into the backyard. Nestled in the pebbles of the driveway was a forlorn mug of brown liquid.

"Maybe," Rose said. Then she tucked the sequin into

the back pocket of her khakis, just in case Lily really was fishy and she needed to prove it later to the police.

"You're a baker, Rose," Ty said, "not a detective."

"Fine," Rose pouted. "Let's bake, then." She laid her marble notebook out on the floor while Ty pulled on the khakis over his lacrosse shorts. "The recipe for love muffins doesn't seem so bad. Here." She pointed to the heading on the recipe:

### Muffins of Green Squash. To Dissolve Love's Various Impediments

"Green squash?" Ty gagged.

"Another name for zucchini," Rose said. Then she read out loud what she'd copied:

It was in 1718 in the British country town of Gosling's Wake that Sir Jasper Bliss brought together two most unfortunate souls, the widower James Corinthian and dressmaker

Petra Biddlebumme, who were too sad and too shy, respectively, to leap into the glorious fire of love. Jasper made a special delivery of these squash muffins to each one's house, then waited a safe distance from the dressmaking shop of Petra Biddlebumme. Two hours past the delivery of the muffins, widower James Corinthian ran to the door of Petra Biddlebumme, who asked him in for tea. They were married one month thence.

"Awww," Ty said sarcastically. "It's like an ancient version of Mr. Bastable and Miss Thistle."

"You're right," Rose said. "You know what we should do to test out the recipe? Bake two of these muffins, give them to Mr. Bastable and Miss Thistle when they come in today, then see if they fall in love!"

Ty got a look on his face like he just bit into a lemon. "Can't we get two *attractive* people together?"

Rose groaned. "You would say that. Listen, the

man wears a frog sweatshirt. At this point, magic is his only hope. Do we have everything for the recipe?"

Ty read the recipe itself out loud:

Sir Jasper Bliss did grate one large green squash while chanting the names of the lonely customers thrice. Sir Jasper did pass through a metal sieve one fist of flour and one fist of sugar. Sir Jasper did drizzle two acorns of the finest distilled Tahitian vanilla over the flour. Then he did fold within the batter one egg of the Masked Lovebird, *Agapornis personata*, which Sir Jasper did acquire from a mystic who had collected them from the primordial forests of Madagascar.

Rose stared up at Ty. "Where are we supposed to find the egg of a masked lovebird? Do we have to go to Madagascar?"

Ty scowled. "I don't know. . . . Mom and Dad have all kinds of weird stuff in the kitchen. They probably have dinosaur eggs."

They walked down into the kitchen and into the walk-in refrigerator to investigate the eggs. Rose opened a brown cardboard carton labeled CALAMITY POULTRY: HAPPY CHICKENS MAKE HAPPY KITCHENS! Inside were a dozen ordinary white eggs—definitely not the eggs of a masked lovebird, whatever those looked like.

"What's this?" Ty said, and Rose stood on her tiptoes to see what he was talking about. Behind stacks of egg cartons was a knob shaped like a rolling pin. "Cool," he said, "I love rolling pins!" He spun it hard with his hand, and a gust of wind blew into the refrigerator, which was already cold enough. Rose felt a sudden warmth at her ankles. She looked at the floor and saw that part of the tiling had slid backward into itself, revealing a wooden staircase that led into a cellar.

A hidden passageway! Rose stared at Ty, who stared

back in disbelief.

"This is, like, the second secret room we found in this refrigerator this *week*," he said.

Rose grabbed a flashlight from a drawer in the kitchen, and she and Ty made their way down the stairs, which were crooked, unfinished planks of wood that seemed ready to collapse at any second. The glow from the flashlight was measly, and Rose could see only a few inches in front of her. She could feel her heart thumping heavily, but Ty's footsteps behind her were steady and calm.

When she got to the bottom of the stairs, Rose shuffled along the cold concrete floor, holding the flashlight up in front of her with shaking hands. She screamed at what she saw.

Staring back at her from inside a blue mason jar was a face, like a human face, only much smaller.

"What is that!?" Ty screamed.

Rose winced and moved the light closer, so that the whole jar came into view. There was, inside the jar, what could only be described as a gnome. It was a little man, about half a foot tall, with a white puffy beard and a green cap. He wasn't dead and shriveled, as you'd expect a gnome to be—he was breathing. Snoring, in fact. He had a dreamy smile on his face and his nostrils flared and then collapsed again as he breathed in and out. Rose was floored. There was a label at the bottom of the jar that read THE DWARF OF PERPETUAL SLEEP.

Ty was speechless for a minute. "No *way*," he said, peering into the jar at the snoring creature.

Rose let the flashlight slide to the right, where another jar sat. This one appeared to be empty, except for a little red leaf that was swirling around inside like it was in the park on a fall day. This jar read THE FIRST WIND OF AUTUMN.

Ty had spun around in the opposite direction to investigate a jar that was filled with a dusty glow. "What's that one?" Rose asked him.

"Light from a lunar eclipse," he whispered. The light cast a blue tint on his nose. He peered at a jar on the shelf beneath it and gasped. "Look, Rose!"

Rose spun around and placed the flashlight in front of a smaller jar. This one was not made of the same shimmering blue-tinted glass as the others— this one was made of green glass that was reinforced with barbed wire. The clasp on the jar was made of heavy rusted metal, and it was locked. Rose could barely make out what was inside—it seemed to be a slimy gray orb, about the size of a baseball. The label read WARLOCK'S EYE.

Rose and Ty turned to each other in disbelief. They'd seen their father chase down wind and whispers and exotic birds—had he slain a warlock, too, and stolen its eye? Were there such things as warlocks? Would the warlock ever be back for its eye? Rose shivered at the thought. If there were Dwarves of Perpetual Sleep living in a secret room beneath the kitchen, what else was there?

Ty tapped Rose on the shoulder and said, "Here, look! Masked lovebird eggs!"

There, in one of the blue jars, were a dozen or so tiny red eggs, flecked with black. Ty grabbed the jar off the shelf and said, "Let's go. I don't want to know what else is down here."

For once, Rose had to admit that she didn't really want to know either.

No sooner had Rose and Ty set out the marble notebook on the kitchen counter than Lily, Sage, and Chip burst through the backdoor, carrying stacks of wooden crates filled with blueberries, strawberries, and raspberries.

"How are we gonna cook with them in here?" Rose asked Ty quietly.

A devilish grin crept across his face. "Let me go talk to Leigh."

He disappeared upstairs, then reappeared, Leigh following wide-eyed in his wake. "It's on," he mouthed silently.

"Hey, guys?" Ty called to Chip and Lily. "Can you

two watch Leigh today? The old *hermana* and I need to concentrate on baking."

Chip approached the glass front door of the bakery. There was already a loud line of hungry townspeople in the early-morning sun, waiting impatiently for their morning pastries: the fibbing dressmaker Mrs. Havegood, the impossibly tall Sheriff Raeburn, the quiet librarian Miss Karnopolis, and a dozen others, all clamoring for baked goods.

As Chip propped the door open, Leigh ran through, screaming, "Hide! Seek! Hide! Seek!" She bounded down the street.

"Leigh!" Chip screamed. "Get back here!"

Lily grabbed Sage by the hand and ran out the door after Leigh. "We'll catch her!" she shouted, already halfway down the block.

Chip called out, "I'll take care of the customers!" He would have no choice but to leave Rose and Ty alone, for the time being.

In the kitchen, Rose opened the marble notebook

on the counter. She was finally going to have a chance to bake something—not just a usual something, but an extraordinary something! From the Cookery Booke! So why were her hands shaking? She felt like she was about to perform a concert for millions of screaming fans—filled with pride and excitement, but also petrified. What if she made a mistake, and everyone booed? Or worse, what if someone got hurt?

*Sir Jasper Bliss did grate one large green squash while chanting the names of the lonely customers thrice.*

Ty washed a zucchini and pushed it up and down along the rough surface of a cheese grater, and wet ribbons of green dribbled into a pile of messy pulp.

"Don't forget to chant!" said Rose.

Ty groaned. "Mr. Bastable and Miss Thistle."

"Louder!"

"Mr. Bastable and Miss Thistle! Mr. Bastable and Miss Thistle!"

Chip poked his head through the saloon doors. He was breathing rapidly, and his face was red and sweaty. The line outside had doubled. "You kids okay?"

"Sure," Ty stuttered, turning red in the cheeks, "we were just . . . trying to remember the words to . . . a rap."

Chip scowled. "Just like your mother, always talking nonsense while you're baking!" He disappeared behind the doors again; Rose and Ty breathed a sigh of relief.

*Sir Jasper did pass through a metal sieve one fist of flour and one fist of sugar.*

Rose furrowed her brow. "A fist. What the heck is a fist?" She made a fist and held it next to her mother's metal measuring cups, which nested neatly inside one another like Russian dolls. Her fist was about the size of one cup.

Ty held up his own fist, which was the size of a grapefruit, then held up the one-cup measure, which was tiny in comparison. "Well, *mujer*," he said, "people were smaller back then. Let's go with one cup." He dipped the cup measure into the burlap sack of flour and shaved off the excess with his finger, then sifted the flour through a metal sieve that looked like a shallow butterfly net.

Then he did fold within the batter one egg of the Masked Lovebird, *Agapornis personata*, which Sir Jasper did acquire from a mystic who had collected them from the primordial forests of Madagascar.

Rose carefully opened the blue mason jar, making sure that Chip didn't see what they were doing. She cracked the egg into the center of the batter, and a yolk the color of a red rose plopped into the white batter.

The yolk began to tremble and shake in the bowl,

then disappeared beneath the batter. It reappeared a second later on the other side of the bowl, then dipped down again, then reappeared. It moved faster and faster until it began circling the dough, kneading the batter into a ball in the middle of the bowl.

And then the yolk exploded in the batter: The mixture crackled and sizzled, sparks of purple and blue shooting up into the air like miniature fireworks and falling back down. Before their eyes, the batter turned a light, delicate shade of pink. Then the noises stopped, the mixture settled, and it was like nothing extraordinary had ever happened.

Rose shivered. These were no Betty Crocker zucchini muffins.

She was finally becoming a kitchen magician. Even Ty wore a look of awe.

Rose and Ty poured the batter into muffin tins and baked them up, guessing when they needed to. *Bake at the heat of six flames* became 325 degrees, the temperature at which their mother usually set the oven, and *for the time of eight songs* became an awkward half-hour or so of singing through all of the Christmas carols they knew.

After they made it through eight songs, Rose and Ty removed a dozen finely puffed brown-and-green-flecked muffins from the oven and set two off to cool.

"What do we do with the rest?" Rose asked.

"I'll get rid of them," Ty said, carrying the rest of the muffins out of the kitchen.

Rose peered over the saloon doors into the front room and saw Mr. Bastable at the front of a long, rowdy line. He shuffled up to the counter, his white hair puffed up like the head of a dandelion. He was wearing a shirt that said I'M A FROG PRINCE. KISS ME.

Rose rushed through the door, holding the hot muffins, and practically shoved Chip off to the side. "Mr. Bastable! Good morning! How can I help you?"

Mr. Bastable stared back at her, confused. "Good morning," he stuttered, making a show of choosing among the pastries. "I'll have . . . a carrot-bran muffin."

Mr. Bastable turned around and noticed Miss Thistle next in line behind him, wearing a brightly colored jogging outfit.

"Miss Thistle!" Rose shouted. "Step right up!"

Miss Thistle looked around and then pointed to herself. "Me?"

"Yes, you!" Rose said. "Step right up to the counter! We're serving two at a time this morning!" Miss Thistle shuffled up to the counter and stood beside Mr. Bastable. They looked at each other for a moment and smiled, then both turned away, red faced.

Rose had seen the same thing at the sixth-grade dances. The pairs that liked each other stood at opposite ends of the room, smiling at each other, then looking at the floor. She was surprised to find that adults did the same thing.

Miss Thistle tried to speak, but it seemed like her throat had closed. "I'd like a carrot-bran muffin," she managed to squeeze out.

"Funny you should both ask for carrot bran,

because we're out of those!" Rose fibbed. Her palms were sweating, and her voice felt weak and unsteady. "But we made a batch of zucchini muffins that are dynamite! Just out of the oven!"

She held up the two muffins, steam still piping out of the tops like chimneys. Mr. Bastable and Miss Thistle both looked at the muffins, wide-eyed, then nodded in tandem.

"Good," Rose said, plopping the muffins into separate white paper bags and handing them off to Mr. Bastable and Miss Thistle. "It's on the house!"

Both walked mechanically out of the shop, then rushed off down the sidewalk in opposite directions, just as Leigh rushed back inside. She zigzagged among the legs of the rest of the customers, who at this point were tapping their feet impatiently and miffed that Mr. Bastable and Miss Thistle had been offered free muffins.

Aunt Lily and Sage came rushing in after Leigh, who had already escaped up the stairs. Rose didn't mind the chaos in the bakery. She was having too much fun with her big brother.

"Rose! Come here!" called Ty from the kitchen.

When Rose popped through the saloon doors, she saw Ty holding a faded pink index card covered with grease stains and their mother's ornate handwriting. "Look at this," he said. "It's a conversion chart. I found it in the freezer."

It read:

*Fist = half cup*
*Flame = 55 degrees Fahrenheit*
*Song = 4 minutes*
*Acorn = teaspoon*
*Walnut = tablespoon*

Rose winced. "This means, when it said one fist of flour, it meant one-half cup, not a full cup!"

"Well, it sure seemed like it was working. If anything, they'll just love each other more." Ty cringed and shivered at the thought of it. "Gross."

Rose winked. "Well, there's only one way to find out."

Three hours later, Rose and Ty sat crouched behind some shrubs on the lawn of Calamity Falls Elementary School, peering into the classroom where Miss Thistle taught her Magic of Science class at summer day camp.

"Where the heck is Mr. Bastable?" Ty spat. "We've been waiting an hour. They should be over at his place by now, slow-dancing in the middle of a frog tank."

In Rose's head, Mr. Bastable would arrive and stand outside the window of Miss Thistle's classroom, wearing a handsome black pinstripe suit and a fashionable haircut. He would knock on the window and say, "Miss Felidia Thistle, I have loved you from the moment I saw you!" Her face would light up and her eyes would gleam with unshed tears of joy. She would climb through the window and walk off with him, arm in arm, leaving the first graders sitting with their jaws open.

The whole scene was very similar to what Rose wished would happen between her and Devin Stetson, if she ever found herself teaching science at a summer camp.

But Mr. Bastable was nowhere to be found.

Rose sighed. "I guess it was 'cause we messed up the measurements." She felt like ripping out her hair, or crying. Or both. "But now that we know what all the measurements mean, we can get it right next time," she ventured, hoping there would be a next time.

"Ech, I don't know," Ty mumbled. "This seems like a waste of time. I just really wanted to show Aunt Lily that I—we—can do magic." Ty stood up again. "And if we can't, then I have more important things to do. Like video games. Or sleep. Get Sage to help you." He brushed the dirt and leaves off the front of his shirt and walked off.

Rose walked home behind him, sighing in defeat.

\* \* \*

That night, Rose sat in the booth with an exhausted and filthy but happy Leigh on her lap.

Aunt Lily sat next to Rose and patted Leigh's head. "I was so worried about you!" she said.

Aunt Lily had prepared pizza for dinner—a beautiful expanse of thin, sweet dough, wonderful tomato sauce, and fresh mozzarella cheese and olives. Chip had opted to return home, exhausted from a day of manning the front room by himself.

Mrs. Carlson waved a finger in Leigh's face. "I'd have found her," she said firmly. "I used to be a spy."

Lily announced that she had to go to the bathroom and disappeared into her guest room in the basement, which was equipped with a tiny sink, shower, and toilet.

The phone rang, and Rose hopped up to answer it. It was her mother.

"Darling!" Purdy cooed.

Rose's pulse quickened. She wanted so badly to confess that she had been in the storeroom and cellar and had copied the recipes and played with magic and tried to get Mr. Bastable and Miss Thistle together. Most of all, she wanted to tell her mother about Aunt Lily's arrival, to ask if Lily was telling the truth about being part of the family, to ask if she was fishy.

But she realized she shouldn't. She could get all of them into trouble—and really, all Lily had done was help out and mind the shop while her parents were away. Was that so bad?

Still, she should say *something* to her parents, right?

Rose opened her mouth, but as soon as the name Aunt Lily popped into her mind, her tongue went limp, as if her mouth couldn't actually form the sentence. Then, before she knew it, the thought disappeared from her head altogether.

"Honey?" Purdy called through the speaker. "Rose? Are you all right?"

"I meant to say something about something, but it flew out of my head. Just tired, I guess." Rose ended the conversation and hung up the phone.

Sage gnawed on his pizza crust like an animal. "Rose, speechless? *That's* a first!"

Lily reappeared and sat down in the booth. Leigh climbed into her lap, and Lily laughed. Rose watched as Aunt Lily joked with Leigh and her brothers, saw the way their eyes lit up whenever she tossed her head back and flashed a smile. It was difficult to imagine a time when Aunt Lily had not been there, helping at the bakery and polishing her motorcycle and softening Chip like you'd soften a stick of butter.

Still, Rose felt a little flutter of unpleasantness in her stomach. It had been there since Lily arrived.

Yes, there was definitely something not right about Lily. Rose felt it in a place in her gut so deep, she'd never known it existed before now—and yet there it was, panging away, sounding an alarm.

This woman had a secret. Something dark, if not outright sinister. And Rose was determined to find out what it was.

# *Recipe the Second: Cookies of Truth*

*A*fter all the lights were out, Rose went down to the guest room in the basement to say good night to Aunt Lily—or at least she told herself that's what she was doing. Really she was going to rifle through Aunt Lily's bags to confirm her suspicions of, well . . . suspiciousness.

Rose tiptoed down the carpeted steps and saw a

ribbon of misty yellow light from beneath the door of the tiny bathroom. The whole basement was filled with steam and the scent of lavender body wash. No wonder Aunt Lily always smelled like a garden.

Lily's suitcase sat open on the little yellow chair in the corner. Rose padded over and looked into the bag. There were a red leather jumpsuit, a blue lace dress, and a tall black bottle labeled MAGIC POTION.

Bingo! The secret to Aunt Lily's mysterious charisma: She was a witch.

Rose hated to think what was in that magic potion—maybe something even worse than a warlock's eye. She carefully uncorked the bottle and cringed, fearing that something horrible would waft out—a howling demon spirit, perhaps? A ghost? A talking bat?

But nothing wafted out except the mild scent of chemicals.

Rose peered over the rim of the bottle. Inside was a goopy white substance. She shook the bottle so that a bit of the stuff landed in her palm. She sniffed it again—Rose had definitely smelled it before, whenever she got close enough to Ty to smell his cheeks. There was no mistaking it: the magic potion was, in fact, acne medication.

So much for Aunt Lily being a witch.

A muffled *thud* came from the front room on the first level of the house.

Rose jumped in the air, threw the bottle of cream back into Aunt Lily's suitcase, and tiptoed back up the stairs to see who, or what, had caused the thud.

The kitchen was still and cold in the gray moonlight, and Rose felt very much alone in her blue nightgown and fuzzy white socks. Rose froze with fear whenever she found herself alone in the dark, so she tended to stay upstairs at night, where there was always some sister or brother or parent nearby. Leigh slept with a night-light, a little smiling ladybug that glowed orange from the wall, and Rose was secretly glad she shared a room with her younger sister—even though she'd never admit it to her parents.

Rose shivered as she remembered the sleeping dwarf in the jar somewhere beneath her feet and wondered whether he ever woke up.

Then the sounds happened again: three of them.

Rose peered over the top of the swinging saloon doors to the front room and saw someone rapping frantically on the front window of the bakery.

Ty plodded downstairs into the darkened kitchen. "Who's outside?" he whispered. "And where did you go after we brushed our teeth?"

"I— I— I—" Rose stuttered, "wanted a glass of water."

"There's water in the bathroom sink," he reminded her.

"The kitchen water tastes better," she said, which was true, but that had nothing to do with why she was currently standing alone in the kitchen. Rose couldn't let her brothers know about her suspicions—they were both too enchanted by their marvelous Aunt Lily.

"Whatever," he said. "I'm gonna go see who's banging on the door."

Rose followed Ty into the front of the bakery.

"Oh no," Ty grumbled. As Rose flicked on the light switch, she could see why: The frantic figure of the local dressmaker, Mrs. Havegood, was tapping on the window, her eyebrows raised so high that they looked like they were trying to crawl into her hair. She was wearing a little red dress with chickens printed all over it and clutched at her purse, which was too tiny to hold anything but a thimble.

"What does she want *this* time?" Ty muttered, opening the door.

Mrs. Havegood stumbled into the room, panting. "Thank goodness you answered! I'd worked myself half into a frenzy!" She was speaking with a proper British accent, which Ty and Rose both knew to be fake. Mrs. Havegood had been born and raised in Calamity Falls, but her accent shifted according to which foreign city she pretended to have lived in the longest. Some weeks it was

Paris, sometimes Berlin, and once Tokyo, which had been awkward. Mrs. Havegood's past was like a kaleidoscope: very colorful, always changing, and a complete illusion.

"I know it's the middle of the night, but I am in crisis!" she cried. "I just found out that I am receiving a very important visitor tomorrow morning!"

"Who? The *president*?" Ty asked, dripping with sarcasm, knowing that whatever answer Mrs. Havegood gave was sure to be a lie.

"Of Cambodia! Yes! However did you know?"

Ty stared at her blankly. "The president of Cambodia is coming to your house for breakfast tomorrow morning? Does Cambodia even *have* a president?"

"Yes, of course!" she retorted. "He and several other *very important* heads of state will be coming over just after breakfast. We shall have tea. And cookies. I need snickerdoodles! Dozens of snickerdoodles! And I need them to be ready by morning!"

"Why are they coming to your house?" Ty asked, egging her on.

Rose turned back to him and whispered, "Stop!" but it was too late.

Mrs. Havegood patted down her messy hair. "I am so glad you asked," she began. "You see, my father was a stunt master, and he once had a television program wherein he traveled the world and communed with dangerous animals. I used to travel with him. One year we went to Cambodia and attempted to tame the rare and lethal black-bearded lynx, which is a very ferocious jungle cat. My father was able to get the lynx to purr on his lap like a little kitten. The Cambodian president was so impressed that he and my father became good friends and hunting partners. He visited us every seven years. And now the time has come for the Cambodian president to again tour the United States, so naturally he will be stopping by for a good old chat and baked goods. So there."

Ty squinted and took one step closer to Mrs. Havegood. Even though Mrs. Havegood was obviously lying through her teeth, Rose knew that Ty wouldn't make fun of her to her face. Their parents had always let Mrs. Havegood ramble on and on—now that their parents were out of town, it was up to Rose and Ty to make sure she felt at home in the Bliss bakery.

"That all sounds swell," Rose said, coming between them. "But everyone is asleep right now. I don't think we'll be able to have the cookies ready until tomorrow afternoon."

"No!" Mrs. Havegood said, trembling. "I need ten dozen snickerdoodles by morning! And for your trouble, I will pay double!"

Rose knew that she and Ty would have to stay up all night in order to produce ten dozen snickerdoodles. "Are you game?" Rose asked.

Ty just shrugged nonchalantly. He regularly stayed up till five in the morning playing video games anyway.

Rose nodded. "All right, Mrs. Havegood. Come back first thing in the morning and pick up your snickerdoodles. It will be an honor to bake cookies for the president of Cambodia."

"Perhaps he will award you a medal! He loves medals," Mrs. Havegood said, bowing and backing out the door. "I'll be back at nine a.m. sharp!"

And then she hustled off into the dark.

Rose and Ty had to tiptoe around the kitchen in socks to avoid waking Aunt Lily, and they had to bake by candlelight in order to avoid rousing Mrs. Carlson, who was very sensitive to light and would notice that the kids were up way past their bedtime.

"This is ludicrous," Ty said as he sat on the counter, his tan, lean arms folded across his chest.

Rose flipped through the index of the Betty Crocker cookbook, looking for snickerdoodles. "Sherbets . . . shortcake . . . shrimp . . . snap peas . . ."

"Wait," he cut in. Rose caught a glimmer of excitement in his eye that was more than just the reflection of flickering candles. "Get the recipes we copied from the book. I'm pretty sure I remember there being one we can use to get back at Mrs. Havegood for being such a crazy liar. Cambodian president? *Please*."

"Ty, we shouldn't use the book just to play games with Mrs. Havegood. That's not what it's for."

"You're right," he said. Then he pursed his lips into a disappointed pout. "It's just . . . since we struck out yesterday, I really want to get back on that baking horse and try again. I . . . love baking."

Rose looked him up and down. Was he serious? Against her better judgment, she nodded. "All right. I'll go get the recipes."

Rose's heart jumped as she made her way upstairs. Ty was probably manipulating her—acting like he was interested in baking in order to exact revenge on Mrs. Havegood. But so what? Did his real motivations matter? It was wrong to trick the desperate and neurotic Mrs. Havegood, but it was wrong to lie, too—and Mrs. Havegood was the worst liar in all of Calamity Falls. Maybe Ty was onto something.

As Rose dug through her underwear drawer for the recipes, Leigh sleeping still as a pebble in her bed, Sage appeared in the door of Rose and Leigh's room. His curly red hair exploded from the top of his head like a firework on the Fourth of July. "What's going on?" he whined. "Where is Ty? Why aren't you guys asleep?"

Rose hid the handwritten recipes behind her back. "Nothing's going on," she said. "Me and Ty are washing dishes downstairs. Just go to sleep—we'll be up in a minute."

Sage's mouth burst open in an excited cry. "Let me help!"

"Since when do you want to wash *dishes*?" she asked. But she already knew the answer—it was since Ty started wanting to wash dishes, which was when Aunt Lily arrived. She had turned everything upside down.

"We don't need your help, Sage," Rose said, maybe a little too harshly. "Just go to bed." If Rose let Sage downstairs to see what they were doing, he was liable to prance loudly around the kitchen and wake up Aunt Lily or Mrs. Carlson.

Sage frowned. "Fine," he said, and he stomped back to his room. Rose felt awful for scolding her little brother, but she wasn't about to let him spoil the all-nighter she'd planned with her big one.

When Rose got back down to the kitchen, she and Ty flipped through the marble notebook and found the recipe he'd recalled:

### Koekjes van Waarheid (Cookies of Truth)

It was in 1618 in the Dutch mining village of Zandvoort that Lady Birgitta Bliss did expose the jewel thief Gerhard Boots by feeding him a Cookie of Truth. He did maintain his innocence during weeping testimonies from his seven victims, all poor farmers for whom the jewels were their family fortune. Then, after eating one of Lady Birgitta's Koekjes van Waarheid, he

did admit to the thefts, even as he struck
himself about the head and shoulders to
make himself stop talking.

"That's perfect for Mrs. Havegood!" Ty exclaimed.
"Maybe after she eats ten dozen of these, she won't
turn up at our house late at night anymore with fake
emergencies."

Lady Birgitta Bliss did combine two fists of
flour with two fists of brown sugar, three
chicken's eggs, and the gentle sleeping breath
of one who has never lied. This proved to be
a mild corrective for the most heinous of
liars, . . .
Etcetera.

"What was that *etcetera* for?" Rose wondered
aloud. When she was copying down the recipe, Ty
had mumbled "Etcetera," saying that the rest of the

instructions were completely obvious stuff, like "let the cookies cool before eating," so Rose just wrote it down that way. Now she wondered if she'd missed anything important.

"Who cares?" Ty grumbled. "The real question is: Who do we know who has never lied?"

Rose thought about whether her own breath would suffice. It might have a few days prior—she'd always despised lying—but the events of the week thus far had spoiled it. Ever since Aunt Lily showed up, Rose had fibbed more than she ever had in her entire life. This realization made her feel . . . dirty.

"I don't know," Rose said finally.

Just then, Ty's head snapped up. "Leigh! Leigh can barely talk, let alone lie!"

Rose and Ty carried one of the blue mason jars that their parents used to trap magical ingredients upstairs to Leigh's bed.

She was sleeping in a little bundle with the covers

wrapped around her like a cheese blintz. Leigh had been congested lately because of her allergies—on that day alone, Rose had wiped snot from her nose eleven times. Her breathing was so labored that every time she inhaled, she sounded like a lawn-mower engine trying to start. It was hardly "gentle sleeping breath," but it would have to do.

Ty held up the mason jar and whispered, "What do I do with this?"

Rose threw her hands in the air. "I don't know, stick it next to her nose?"

Ty took one look at the little gobs of snot in Leigh's nostril that trembled and shook with each breath, then handed the jar to Rose. "I can't."

"Fine," said Rose, "I'll do it." She held the open jar over her sister's growling, snuffling exhaust pipe of a nose and waited.

The snoring was so powerful that it shook the metal clasp on the jar. After a few breaths, the jar fogged up and Rose gently clasped the lid shut.

"Got it," Rose whispered, and they snuck back downstairs.

Rose and Ty had gotten the knack of the Bliss Cookery Booke measurements, so they multiplied the recipe by ten to make ten dozen—that was ten cups of flour, ten cups of brown sugar, and thirty eggs. They tossed the ingredients in the biggest metal mixing bowl they could find, while the jar with Leigh's breath trapped inside rattled around on the countertop with the sound of her snores.

Just as Ty scooped out the final cup of sandy brown sugar, the jar rattled so heavily that it fell over on its side and rolled off the side of the countertop. Rose threw her body under the counter like she was sliding into home plate, and the jar landed with a *thud* in her lap.

Ty looked at Rose incredulously. "Nice catch, *mi hermana*!" he exclaimed, and he held up his hand for a high five. She slapped his hand and blushed with pride. He hadn't high-fived Rose since before she knew what a high five was.

As soon as Ty had cracked the final egg into the

bowl, it was time for magic. Nothing happened at first as Rose opened the jar over the batter, but after a moment the foggy sides of the jar cleared and congealed into misty little blobs in the center of the jar. Then the honest breath bombs dropped down into the batter and sank to the bottom, then bubbled to the top again like a gurgling swamp. The dough burbled and hissed and spat out gas. The dough suddenly smelled like mustard and pastrami.

"Gross," Ty said. "*That* was in our little sister's breath?"

"Twelve counterclockwise stirrings with a bone spoon," Rose said. Their plastic spoon would have to do. She put some muscle into turning the ever-thickening gloop. As Rose stirred, the batter itself seemed to snore—it expanded and contracted, like it had lungs of its own. One moment it would bubble up as though about to overflow the bowl, and the next it would calm back down into a polite wet wad. It was almost like the dough was alive.

"This is disgusting," Rose said to Ty.

"I think it's pretty rad," Ty whispered.

After three turns, the awful deli smell had disappeared, and after seven turns, the batter had smoothed out into a thick brown soup. With each subsequent turn, the color of the batter lightened—dark chocolate to milk chocolate to a light buttery color, to almost white. After twelve turns, it looked just like cookie dough, and smelled like it, too: sweet and sugary.

Rose and Ty spooned little dollops of the batter onto cookie sheets—ten sheets in total—and popped them into the big oven. It was four in the morning at this point, and Rose couldn't remember ever being so tired. Even Ty was yawning. When the kitchen timer dinged, they took the cookies out, set them on the counter to cool, and stumbled upstairs, thoroughly exhausted.

"Set your alarm for 7:45 a.m.!" Rose told Ty.

"Sure thing, Sis," he mumbled.

"We have to personally hand over those cookies to Mrs. Havegood!" But he had already disappeared into his room, and soon enough Rose was wrapped in her blankets and lost in sleep.

When Rose woke, she was being tossed back and forth as if by a giant ocean wave. She opened her eyes, frightened, and saw Sage and Leigh bouncing up and down on either side of her bed.

"Rose! Rose!" cried Sage. "Wake up! Chip says you have to play with us because we're not being helpful in the kitchen!"

Leigh kicked Rose in the ribs by accident, and Rose let out a cry. She turned and looked at the little electric clock she kept by her bed and gasped.

11:14 a.m.

"Get off!" she screamed at Sage and Leigh, and she tossed away the covers and ran into Ty's room. He was still sleeping.

Rose galloped downstairs, her heart pounding. Chip was bustling around the kitchen. "Well, *there* you are!" he said gruffly.

Just then, Aunt Lily came out from the walk-in fridge, wearing pinstripe pants and a pinafore, carrying several cartons of eggs. Her hair looked bright, black, and shiny. "Rose, darling!"

"Why didn't anyone wake me up?" Rose said.

"We thought we'd let you sleep in! You've been working so hard!"

Then Rose noticed that the trays of cookies were gone, all ten of them. "Did Mrs. Havegood come by for cookies?" Rose asked, praying that all had gone according to plan.

"You bet," answered Chip. "Said something about needing cookies for the prime minister of Fiji." Mrs. Havegood sometimes had trouble keeping her own lies straight.

Rose breathed a sigh of relief.

"But," he began again, "she didn't want them. She said, 'I want snickerdoodles, and these are most certainly *not* snickerdoodles!'" Chip had raised his voice to an airy, grating soprano in order to imitate Mrs. Havegood.

Lily laughed a deep, throaty laugh. "Oh, Chip!"

Rose sighed with disappointment. Had she woken up when she was supposed to, she could have explained to Mrs. Havegood that the cookies were actually a special type of snickerdoodle prized in Southeast Asia. As it was, however, Mrs. Havegood had rejected her cookies. All of that hard work gone to waste. Ty would be so disappointed.

"So you threw them out?" asked Rose.

"Oh, no," Chip replied with a smile. "I would never waste food like that! I gave them away."

Rose's eyes went wide. "You . . . *what?*"

"Sure. I gave everyone a free cookie with their order," answered Chip.

"People couldn't get enough of them!" Lily chimed in. "Whoopee!"

Rose gulped. Oh no! She hadn't been awake more than ten minutes, but she'd already helped poison the whole town with Cookies of Truth.

This was not going to be pretty.

CHAPTER 8

## Truth and Consequences

ose sat down hard on the floor.

She hadn't meant to, but her knees gave way, and when your knees give way, you just sit wherever you are.

"What's wrong, darling?" Lily lilted, a look of concern on her perfectly pretty face. For an instant, Rose was extremely jealous—why did Aunt Lily always look so beautiful? Rose, on the other hand, didn't even need to look in a mirror—she was sure that her own cheeks were red and flushed, her forehead was sweaty, and her eyes were still squinty from sleep.

Sometimes life really wasn't fair.

Chip looked down at her and said, "You want a chair?"

Chip had given out 120 of the magical cookies that were intended only for Mrs. Havegood. Was that so bad? The instructions had said that the *Koekjes van Waarheid* would prove a "mild corrective for the most heinous liars," and Mrs. Havegood was the only truly heinous liar she knew.

Although . . . Rose had become something of a heinous liar herself in the past few days: She'd lied to Aunt Lily, she'd lied to Chip, she'd lied to Mr. Bastable and Miss Thistle, and worst of all, she'd lied to her parents.

Yes, if Rose had eaten one of the Cookies of Truth, she'd be toast. But the rest of Calamity Falls should be safe enough. Right?

"Rose!" Sage called. "Come play with us!"

Sage and Leigh were bouncing on the trampoline in the backyard while Mrs. Carlson sat nearby in a lawn chair, sipping an iced tea and watching a soap opera on her portable TV, a sad little cube with rabbit-ear antennae that she'd likely been toting around since the mid-1980s.

"The kids have been asking for you all morning!" said Aunt Lily. Normally this would have made Rose feel a certain pride, but at the moment it felt like a nuisance.

"Not now!" Rose screamed out the door. Then she turned politely to Chip. "Who exactly did you give the cookies to?"

Chip folded his massive arms across his chest and squinted. "What is this, twenty questions? Were the cookies poisoned? What's the big deal?"

Aunt Lily gently touched Chip's massive shoulder and he relaxed. "Now, Chipper . . ."

Rose improvised. "Well, they had some . . . pulverized pecan dust in them, and I just want to make sure you didn't give them to anyone with a nut allergy."

Chip smiled and began again. "I understand. I gave some to Mr. Bastable the frog sweatshirt guy, and Miss Thistle the teacher—all the teachers, actually—and the men's golf association, and the bankers, and the doctor, and the hairdresser. People really loved them. But don't worry—I kept a few for the family," he said, indicating a platter of the little brown nuggets sitting on the counter.

"You're sure that's everybody?"

Chip took a deep breath and scratched his bald head. "Let me think. Who else?" A thick blue vein in Chip's forehead pulsed like a river. "Aha!" he cried. "A bunch of librarians came by. They were all on a yellow school bus."

"Oh," said Rose. "The Triple L."

Chip and Lily looked at Rose, puzzled.

"The League of Lady Librarians. They take field trips all over town once a week. Sometimes they go to the museum, sometimes they go to the park, sometimes they go horseback riding, and sometimes they come here. Mom loves them."

"They were nice gals," Chip said. "Real polite."

Rose was about to ask him again if that was *everyone* he'd given cookies to when there was a screeching sound outside. Rose turned her head and stared out one of the large windows: A yellow school bus with the letters *LLL* painted on the side in electric blue squealed to a halt right in front of the bakery, nearly crashing into a line of parked cars.

The high-school librarian, Mrs. Canterbury, emerged from the bus, her bangs wet with sweat and her cheeks flushed. Mrs. Canterbury bustled through the door and up to the counter.

Rose pushed through the saloon doors into the front room to greet her.

"Hello, young Rose," Mrs. Canterbury began in a worried whisper. "The Ladies would like more of the little brown cookies that were given away here earlier. I personally cannot eat sweets, so I didn't partake of the cookies—no offense—but they enjoyed them very, very much and told me that if I didn't come back with three dozen more right away, they would 'punch my lights out.'"

"That doesn't sound like a very Triple-L thing to say," Rose ventured.

"They're a little . . . on edge today," said Mrs. Canterbury, glancing back at the bus. Librarians in their blazers and V-neck sweaters had their faces pressed to the windows of the bus, staring maniacally into the bakery.

Rose had never seen anything like it. Perhaps the *Koekjes van Waarheid* were to blame, but how could they be? They were supposed to affect only "the most heinous liars," which the ladies of the Triple L were most certainly *not*.

Or were they?

"Hurry, please!" Mrs. Canterbury said. "I'm worried. The Ladies aren't themselves today."

Another librarian burst forth from the bus. Rose

recognized her as Miss Karnopolis, who used to read stories aloud during library time in elementary school. She had taken her hair down from its usual French twist and it was flying around her head in a frizzy mane.

"Good morning!" screeched Miss Karnopolis. "Or *is* it? My face itches and I have not had a successful encounter with a bathroom in three days now! So I suppose it is, in fact, a so-so morning. A mediocre morning at best! And the bizarre décor in here is not helping matters one bit! I mean, *stripes*? Is this a bakery or a circus tent?"

"Augustine, please!" hushed Mrs. Canterbury.

"*Please* yourself, Pat!" Miss Karnopolis snapped. "It's about time someone told the truth about this place. Whoever picked the wallpaper in this room should be slapped!"

Chip stepped out into the front room, the vein in his forehead pulsing like the throat of a groaning frog. "*I* picked the wallpaper," he growled.

Lily burst in after him. "It's great wallpaper, Chippy," she said. "At least, as far as wallpaper goes." She turned to Miss Karnopolis. "I've always preferred a nice coat of paint."

But Miss Karnopolis wasn't paying Aunt Lily any attention—instead, her jaw had dropped at the sight of Chip and his muscle-bound chest. "Oh my," Miss Karnopolis stammered. "Oh *my*, my, my. Oh ME, oh me, oh my. Oh. My."

Chip gulped and started backing through the saloon doors. "Never mind," he said, the doors swinging in front of him.

Aunt Lily stifled a giggle, then turned her attention back to the unfolding drama, somehow managing to stay cool.

"Augustine! What on earth has gotten into you?" Mrs. Canterbury pleaded.

Miss Karnopolis leaned over the countertop and pulled Rose close. "Rose, your hair is nice. You should be satisfied with it—as long as it doesn't fall out in your old age. Your face, taken by itself, is not as pretty as your brother Thyme's face is handsome. What I mean is that if Thyme were a girl, he would be prettier than you, and if you were a boy, you would be less handsome than Thyme."

Rose was horrified. This was something she sometimes worried about in the privacy of her own head when she was falling asleep—it never occurred to her that other people might be thinking it as well, let alone her beloved elementary-school librarian.

Rose coughed and said, "Um, thanks."

Aunt Lily put a reassuring hand on Rose's shoulder. "Don't worry, my pet," Lily said. "You have something that Ty doesn't have."

Before Rose could ask what Lily was talking about, ten angry librarians came stomping into the bakery, setting off a cacophony of jingling from the bells that hung from the door handle.

The librarians stood in groups of twos and threes and argued back and forth about anything and

everything. Mrs. Hackett, Calamity Falls adult fiction specialist, and Mrs. Crisp, Calamity Falls adult
reference specialist, began a shouting match near the
counter.

"You couldn't archive scholarly articles if you
tried!" yelled Mrs. Crisp.

"Oh, peacock poop!" Mrs. Hackett retorted.

It went on like that, the din in the front room
growing unbearable. Chip peeked worriedly over the
tops of the saloon doors.

"I'm sure they're all just having a bad day," Rose
told him, even though she knew it was much more
than that.

Mrs. Hackett and Mrs. Crisp drifted over to the
far-right counter, where the Bliss family displayed all
of the seven-layer cakes they made, a Bliss specialty:
coconut cream, pineapple, chocolate, banana, carrot, strawberry shortcake, and a moist, pecan-riddled
tower that Purdy had named, simply, Heaven. The
cakes sat on white porcelain stands, covered by glass

domes with little red knobs on top.

"Admit it, Crisp," said Mrs. Hackett. "You don't take me seriously! Just because I'm not a reference nerd, like you!"

Mrs. Crisp turned up her nose. "I would rather be a reference nerd than an expert in *romance novels*!"

Every member of the League of Lady Librarians gasped and stopped their fighting. They turned to Mrs. Hackett and Mrs. Crisp and watched, terrified.

"What did you say?" Mrs. Hackett asked in a hushed growl.

"You heard me," said Mrs. Crisp, her lower lip trembling.

Mrs. Hackett reached over, pulled the glass dome off the seven-layer coconut-cream cake, picked it up, and shoved the cake into Mrs. Crisp's face—all seven layers.

Mrs. Crisp was speechless, her eyes and hair and entire face covered with a layer of thick white icing, flecked with strands of white coconut. She licked a blob off her lips and said, "I don't like coconut."

Then a volcano of sound erupted as all of the librarians shrieked and screamed and clawed at one another. Mrs. Canterbury cowered behind the wrought-iron café table to shield her eyes, while Miss Karnopolis stormed behind the counter and pelted her with blueberry muffins. Mrs. Hackett and Mrs. Crisp were wrestling on the floor in the smeared remains of the coconut-cream cake, while others stood in a circle around them and cheered.

Sage and Leigh ran in from the backyard to watch, and Mrs. Carlson ran after them. "Animals!" she said. The fight woke up Ty as well, and he staggered into the front room, rubbing sleep from his eyes.

"Chip gave our cookies away to the Triple L," Rose hissed. "I think they worked."

The corners of Ty's mouth raised just a little bit. "Cool," he said.

But it wasn't cool, Rose thought. It was dangerous.

"I'll save the littl'uns!" Mrs. Carlson shouted as she

herded Sage and Leigh out of the kitchen and upstairs.

A moment later, Chip came to the rescue. He burst through the doors wielding a cordless electric beater and a crème brûlée torch like they were jousting weapons. "Enough!" he shouted, whirring the beaters and igniting the torch. A jet of blue flame shot into the air.

The librarians stopped fighting and backed toward the exit, muttering to one another about how Chip was handsome as the devil but not really the life of the party. When the last one was back on the bus, Chip nervously locked the front door of the bakery.

"I think it's best to close up shop for the day," he said, sounding deeply shaken. Whatever horrors he'd seen as a fighting marine didn't hold a crème brûlée torch to the cake-flinging war that had just broken out in the shop.

"Let's clean up this mess, Chip," said Lily.

"That's a good idea," said Rose. "I'll help in a minute. I just need to get something from the walk-in." And she dragged Ty deep into the depths of the fridge.

\* \* \*

Rose and Ty frantically flipped through the pages of the Bliss Cookery Booke and found the recipe for the Cookies of Truth. In the margins was an etching of a scene much like the one they had just witnessed: men and women in wooden clogs and double-pointed Dutch hats throwing loaves of bread in each other's faces and screaming at one another.

Rose found the passage she'd been looking for:

*Lady Birgitta Bliss did combine two fists of **flour** with two fists of **brown sugar**, three **chicken's eggs**, and the **gentle sleeping breath of one who has never lied**. This proved to be a mild corrective for the most heinous of liars.\**

But there was no "etcetera"—it was an asterisk.

At the bottom of the page she found a note hidden in the filigree of the illustration. It was very hard to make out the writing, particularly by the light of the miniature flashlight that Rose had stuffed in her pocket, but she got the gist of it.

*When administered with a glass of milke. Without the coating of milk from cow, sheep, goat, or cat, not only will the tongues of liars be corrected, but all the venom wisely restricted by the tongues of the merely polite will be unloosed. Chaos will reign.*

"Ty! You told me this stuff wasn't important! It's *very* important!"

"Harsh, Rosita. *Mucho* harsh," he said. "I'm going back to bed." He glanced at her before shutting the door and said, "It's like I can't do anything right. You sound just like Mom."

At that, Rose shuddered. She knew exactly how he felt.

Rose shut the book and rushed out of the library, barely remembering to lock the door, then ran out of the fridge, knocking over a very tall woman in long pinstripe pants and a pinafore.

Rose stood up and brushed herself off, panting.

Aunt Lily.

Aunt Lily had been leaning against the fridge, waiting. Her face was a mixture of makeup and mystery. "Care to tell me what you've been doing in there?" she asked.

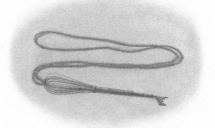

## CHAPTER 9
### *Love from On High*

L ily repeated her question: "What were you up to
in there, Rose? Your color is all gone."

Rose turned and surveyed her reflection in the gray
steel of the walk-in fridge and saw that her skin was, in
fact, the color of dental floss.

"I was just . . . getting a glass of orange juice," Rose
lied.

Lily knelt down and touched Rose's cheek and

said, "Rose, you were in there for ten minutes, and you haven't brought out any juice. And you're freezing!" She wrapped her arms around Rose. "Sit here on my knee."

Rose lowered herself onto the thigh of her fake aunt's gray pinstripes and sat there awkwardly, like a child on a mall Santa.

"Now, tell me the truth," Lily said gently. "What are you hiding back there, behind that tapestry?"

Rose tried to hide her surprise. How did Lily know there was something behind that tapestry? She *must* have eavesdropped on Rose and Ty and Sage arguing back and forth as they copied down the recipes the morning before, when Rose found a purple sequin from Lily's pants on the floor of the fridge.

Rose wanted to tell her aunt about the book and the Love Muffins gone wrong and the Cookies of Truth gone, unfortunately, *right*—but her parents had told her to protect the secret of the Bliss Cookery Booke, and she had to obey her parents.

So instead of spilling her guts, Rose countered with an equally important question: "Why were you eavesdropping on us yesterday morning?"

Aunt Lily looked her straight in the eye, and Rose stared right back, marveling at the dark glimmer of Lily's brown eyes and the jaunty ramp of her eyelashes, which were so long that they looked like the kind of eyelashes a woman in a cartoon bats for attention. "I eavesdropped because I was worried, Rose. The three of you, getting up that early to hang out in a refrigerator, and then staying up all night to make cookies—"

Rose barely managed a whisper: "But we were so quiet!"

Lily laughed. "Rose! I am a creature of the night." She patted Rose on the head like Rose was five and not twelve. Rose hated that. "Now, I appreciate your enthusiasm for baking, I really do. You are a natural. But if you are doing all this sneaking around because you're in some kind of trouble, or because you're hiding a secret . . ."

Rose's pulse quickened and she felt a movement in her throat, the kind you feel when you're about to vomit up either the truth or your dinner. Aunt Lily was too smart. There was no hiding anything from her.

"Maybe a secret that someone else asked you to keep. A friend, maybe, or . . . a parent."

Rose twitched.

"An adult should never ask a child to keep one of their secrets," Lily said gravely. "It isn't fair." She gave Rose's shoulder a squeeze.

Rose was about to come out with it, the whole thing. Lily was right: It wasn't fair for her parents to ask Rose to keep this tremendous secret—not just the secret of the locked-away Cookery Booke, but the secret of their family magic. Rose had been hiding it her whole life. The only people she could ever tell about the lightning in the bottle or the clouds or the nightingale or the warlock's eye were her brothers, and they didn't care. Her parents had made it so that she could never really be honest with *anyone*.

"I—I—I—" Rose began.

A look of impatience flashed over Lily's face—it was a subtle narrowing of her eyes and crinkling of her eyebrows. It passed like the shadow of a quickly moving cloud, but it lingered just long enough to make Rose hold her tongue.

What was it about Aunt Lily that made Rose suspicious? Until she figured out what that was, she couldn't expose her family's secret.

"Behind that tapestry is another refrigerator where my parents keep the really good chocolate," said Rose. "We snuck in there the other morning and ate some. It was wrong of us. So I locked it, and I'm holding the key so Ty and Sage can't get in there again." Rose exhaled so hard that she coughed, then got up off her fake aunt's knee.

Lily stood up too. "Thank you for being honest," she said, a little gruffly.

A moment of uncomfortable silence was broken when Leigh and Sage ran into the kitchen and began jumping up and down, rattling all the pots and pans.

"Mrs. Carlson fell asleep in front of her little TV," Sage said, the words getting lost amid his jumps.

"Stop jumping, guys," said Rose.

"I can't!" cried Sage. "I've been doing it for so long, I can't stop! I have to eat something to weigh me down!"

"What do you two want to eat?" Lily asked.

Sage was about to answer when Leigh cut in. "Snails!" she shouted.

"Ugh!" Sage dropped to the floor and squirmed around, gagging. Rose knew that his fear and hatred of snails and slugs was not an exaggeration, and that the very mention of them really did make him gag.

Lily herself looked a little disgusted. "She wants snails from the garden?" she ventured.

"No," answered Rose. "She wants escargots. We have to go to Pierre Guillaume's French bistro." Rose was used to this weekly ritual. It was strange that a three-year-old should love eating escargots so much, but ever since the first time Leigh popped one of the rubbery, garlicky, buttery snails into her mouth, there was no stopping her. "Leigh has to have escargots once a week, or she gets very grumpy."

Lily's face lit up. "A French bistro?" she cried, pronouncing the *r* in *bistro* the way the French would— that is, almost coughing. "Say no more!"

Then Aunt Lily noticed Sage, who was still writhing in disgust on the floor. "What about Sage?"

"Sage," Rose answered, smoothing his curly red mop, "will sit on the other end of the table and avert his eyes."

In her bedroom, Rose put on her favorite dress, a simple blue one with a skirt that started practically at the collar. She wasn't sure that she felt pretty—her eyebrows were too dark, her nose was too stubby—but when she was wearing the dress she at least felt prett*ier*. Pretty*ish*.

Then she helped Leigh change out of the filthy

red-and-white-striped shirt she wore every day and put on her freshly washed backup red-and-white-striped shirt, which Albert and Purdy kept on hand for whenever Leigh had to look presentable. She insisted on bringing her Polaroid camera.

Meanwhile, Aunt Lily went downstairs to consult the wardrobe in her seemingly bottomless suitcase and emerged looking extra Parisian, wearing a blue-and-white-striped T-shirt and a black beret that dangled to one side of her head. Chip kept on the shirt that he'd been wearing, and Sage saw fit to wear the baggy blue T-shirt that he'd been sweating in all morning. All in all, they looked optimistic, if not fabulous.

Except for Aunt Lily, who would look fabulous even in a burlap sack.

Aunt Lily popped on a pair of fancy sunglasses and spread both her arms wide into the air. "Off we go! The bakery is closed for the day, and we are taking a holiday!" It seemed she could make a holiday out of anything.

Rose and Lily held on to Leigh's hands and swung her back and forth like an orangutan toward the town square while Chip and Sage trailed behind.

Rose looked over at her aunt, who had her face turned to the sun and seemed to be savoring every second of daylight like it was vanilla pudding.

"Do you know how I feel right now, Rose?" Lily said, smiling.

Rose shook her head no.

"I feel insouciant." Lily stretched out the foreign-sounding word like it was a piece of toffee: *innnnn . . . soooooo . . . seeeeee . . . annnnnntttt*. "See, in French, *souci* means *worry*. So *in*souciant means *without worry*, without care. I am without a care! Isn't that just delicious?"

Chip chimed in from where he was marching five feet behind them. "In that case, I am also insouciant."

Rose relaxed her shoulders, which she had been keeping scrunched up near her ears for the past few hours. The soft cotton of her flowing skirt brushed up against her legs in the breeze like a cat looking to get fed, and she felt, for a moment, like all would be well. A few overly frank librarians were not the worst things in the world. The cookies would wear off sooner or later, and everything would go back to normal, including Rose, who would once again resume her position as the girl who quietly did everything right.

A moment later they swung into the town square, an open plaza made of terra-cotta bricks that practically glowed in the sun. In the center of the plaza was a marble statue of the town's founder, Reginald Calamity, milking a cow. In summertime, the statue served as a fountain, and streams of water poured out of the cow's udder. Rose thought that was tasteless, and that the Calamity Falls Civic Association should get a new statue, one with less . . . milking.

Lily stood near the statue for a minute and stared up at it. "Interesting."

As they swung past the statue toward the café

tables of Pierre Guillaume's, Rose saw a line of about fifty people waiting outside the restaurant.

"What the heck?" Rose said. "Since when do you need a reservation at Pierre Guillaume's?"

Then Rose noticed that the people weren't so much in a line as they were bunched together in a noisy crowd, and that everyone in the crowd was staring upward to the top of the restaurant, where Pierre Guillaume had, a few months ago, installed a four-story steel replica of the Eiffel Tower.

Then Rose saw what everyone was looking at.

Mr. Bastable was scaling Pierre Guillaume's fake Eiffel Tower.

He had somehow managed to get to the roof of the restaurant—probably by use of the ladder that was leaning against the building—and was now climbing, rung by rung, up the tower. Around them, the towns-people were calling out, "Mr. Bastable! Don't do it!" and "Come back down!" but he ignored them.

Pierre Guillaume came out of his restaurant in his

white chef's coat and hat to greet the crowd. *"Ooh la la!"* he squealed. "I have never had so many customers! Some of you may have to wait, but worry not! I shall serve one and all. . . ." He trailed off when he realized that the crowd gathered outside his restaurant had nothing to do with his food. He turned and looked up and quietly repeated himself: "Ooh la la."

Rose's pulse quickened. Did this daring stunt have anything to do with the cookie that Chip had served Mr. Bastable? Was it because of yesterday's muffin? Was this the natural result of two magical recipes churning in the stomach of a shy frog enthusiast?

Pierre Guillaume was near tears. *"Monsieur! Monsieur! Excusez-moi!* You cannot climb up there! My fake Tour Eiffel will not hold your weight! *Monsieur!* You are climbing to your death!"

But Mr. Bastable continued, undaunted.

Pierre Guillaume, in a panic, ran toward the firehouse two blocks down. "Help! Help! The frog man is on my tower!"

Mr. Bastable finally reached the top. He wrapped his skinny arms and legs around the fake steel beams and clung with all his might as a gust of wind blew past him, whipping his puffy white hair against his cheeks.

He gazed down at the crowd, clearly terrified, and then up at the sky. Rose hoped that he had just gone crazy on his own, and it had nothing to do with cookies or muffins or Miss Thistle.

But then he began to shout.

"I, Bernard Bastable, am in love with Miss Felidia Thistle!"

Rose cringed. It was worse than she'd feared. The Love Muffins and the Cookies of Truth had combined into a powerful spell all its own.

"I want to nibble on her lady fingers!" he shouted, a broad smile on his face. "Oh, I want to kiss her nose and bake her a pie! I want to put some pie on her nose and lick it off!" Everyone in the crowd groaned and looked away, embarrassed.

"Felidia Thistle is the most sensational creature in this town—or in any town, for that matter! I want to watch her stomp grapes! She will be my queen!" As he said this, Mr. Bastable threw both his arms wide, and the tower creaked and leaned a bit to the right. He winced and hugged the tower again.

But no one was watching him anymore. Everyone had turned their attention to the marble statue of Reginald Calamity, where Miss Thistle was staring at the roof of Pierre Guillaume's like someone had crashed a bus on it.

Mr. Bastable spied Miss Thistle standing there in front of the fountain. "Felidia!" he shouted. "You are my darling, my peach pie, my sweet crumpet! My only, my one true! Say you love me too!"

It seemed as though Miss Thistle was about to say something, but she clapped her hands over her mouth so that whatever she yelled got trapped in her teeth.

Clinging to the tower with only his legs, Mr. Bastable pulled off his frog sweatshirt to reveal a skimpy white undershirt. The words MARRY ME! were printed across the front in red paint.

"Felidia! Let me be your frog prince!" he yelled again.

Miss Thistle started to shout, "I—," but again muffled herself, this time by pulling the neck of her gray turtleneck over her head.

Then Mr. Bastable did something truly embarrassing: While holding tight to the tower with one hand, he unbuttoned his slacks with the other, then dropped his pants into a rumpled pile atop the roof of Pierre Guillaume's.

In his red polka-dotted boxer shorts, Mr. Bastable scooted around so that his bottom was facing the crowd. There was a phrase painted on the back of the boxers: "NO IFS, ANDS, OR BUTTS!"

"It's disgusting," Chip muttered.

Leigh was cackling like she'd never cackled before.

Sage looked like he might vomit.

Aunt Lily turned to Rose. "You've got to applaud

his enthusiasm," she said.

But Rose was looking the other way, at Miss Thistle, who was shaking her head so violently that her glasses had fallen into the fountain.

"Bernard Bastable!" Miss Thistle shouted, finally. "I love you too! I want to make you my frog prince! Never in all my years have I seen a man with such magnificent, froglike charisma! You are a treasure! Kiss me now!"

As she finished, Miss Thistle crossed her eyes and covered her mouth again, horrified, as if it had betrayed her. She turned and ran away toward the schoolhouse, her face purple with embarrassment.

"Come back, sweet Felidia!" Mr. Bastable cried.

A siren pealed out as the Calamity Falls Fire Department engine careened through the town square. "There!" Pierre Guillaume shouted, pointing. "That man is going to break my Eiffel Tower!"

The crowd made room for the truck as it eased to a halt in front of the restaurant.

Fire Chief Conklin squinted up at Mr. Bastable and raised a megaphone. "Bernard Bastable! If you do not get down immediately, we will have to come up there and remove you!"

Mr. Bastable shook his head. "Not until my Ladylove agrees to be my Lady Wife!"

Two firemen unfolded a forty-foot metal ladder and set it against the top of the tower. "What's that guy *on*?" the one fireman asked the other.

Rose gulped. She knew exactly what he was on. And it was all her fault. What would her parents do if they were there? Surely they'd have a way to fix this. Although, really, they would never have gotten themselves into this mess to begin with.

It was only after Mr. Bastable had safely been dragged down the ladder that the tower groaned and teetered in the wind.

"Oh no," Rose said.

"Oh yes," Sage said, his eyes wide with excitement. "That tower is coming down! Tim-*berrrrrrrrrrr!*"

Leigh pointed her camera toward the roof and clicked.

Another wind gusted hard, and with a mighty *crack* the tower wobbled and fell over in slow motion, coming down right toward the crowd.

"Everybody *move!*" Chip yelled, scooping up Leigh in one arm and Sage in the other and running to the right. The townspeople scattered to either side as the tower crashed down against the square, folding up with a metallic clatter right in the front of the restaurant.

"Nooooo!" cried Pierre Guillaume, burying his head in his hands and beginning to sob.

Rose felt someone poking at her shoulder, and she turned around to see Ty, who was running a hand through his hair to make sure it looked just the right kind of messy.

"What's going on?" he muttered, unimpressed by all the mayhem. "I came downstairs from my nap and everyone had vamoosed." Ty was dressed in a pair of jeans that was only slightly wrinkled and a long-sleeved navy blue shirt.

"I need to speak with you," Rose whispered, pulling Ty away toward the fountain. "Mr. Bastable and Miss Thistle both went bonkers. Mr. Bastable scaled the fake Eiffel Tower and declared his love for Miss Thistle, and Miss Thistle couldn't help but shout it back. The combination of Love Muffins and Cookies of Truth is lethal! We need to figure out a way to fix this, immediately, before Aunt Lily catches on, and before word gets back to Mom and Dad that the town is going crazy!"

Ty gulped. "Oh."

"What now?" Rose said, rolling her eyes.

"It might be even worse than that," Ty began slowly, looking a bit sheepish. "I *may* have taken those extra Love Muffins and given them"—he paused for another gulp—"to a couple of girls in my class."

## CHAPTER 10

# You Scream, I Scream

*A*s far as everyone else was concerned, the excitement was over.

The crowd that had gathered to watch Mr. Bastable had scattered. A few old ladies took a seat on the ledge of the Reginald Calamity fountain and talked about how it would be nice if some man had climbed a tower to proclaim his love for *them*. A few men sipped coffee and complained that in the old days towers weren't built so flimsily. Lily and Chip stood next to the maitre d's podium outside Pierre Guillaume's chattering about the things on the menu they wanted to eat. And Pierre Guillaume was crying as a noisy yellow crawler crane lifted the cracked remains of the tower high into the air and dropped them into a rusty red Dumpster.

Rose and Ty stood under the shadow of the awning of the law offices of Karen Publickson, Esq., trying to figure out what to do.

Through the window, Rose could see Ms. Publickson sitting calmly at a desk, looking natty in a navy business suit with her black hair perfectly arranged in a twist on the back of her head. *Maybe I should be a lawyer instead of a magical baker*, Rose thought. *Lawyers' mistakes rarely result in old men climbing on top of towers and taking off their pants.*

Rose's lips were pursed so tight in anger that she could barely speak. "Ty," she managed to squeeze out, "*why* did you give girls in your class Muffins of Love and Cookies of Truth?"

Ty just shrugged. He was looking annoyingly pleased with himself.

Rose wanted to smack him over the head—despite the fact that if she had been presented with the opportunity to give Devin Stetson both a Love Muffin and a Cookie of Truth, she probably would have shoved them down his throat faster than he could say thank you.

Before Ty could answer, the calm hum of the sun-drenched brick plaza was broken by a horrible shriek. It sounded like a girl was being mugged, but no one had ever been mugged in the entire history of Calamity Falls, much less in the blinding daylight of the town square.

It was Lindsey Borzini. She was running toward the law offices of Karen Publickson—or rather, toward Ty. "There he is!" she howled. "It's— It's— TY!"

Lindsey, the oldest daughter of Mr. Borzini, peanut-shaped proprietor of Borzini's Nuttery, was known for having the worst tan in Calamity Falls.

As she shrieked and careened across the brick plaza toward Ty, she looked like a roasted carrot with arms.

She was waving a thin, glossy book in the air with one hand and a Sharpie marker with the other. Was it an issue of *Tiger Beat*? Had Ty recently put out a pop album that Rose didn't know about?

As she got closer, Rose saw that it was the Calamity Falls Middle School yearbook. Ty had graduated from there in June, and lumped in with the other eighth graders was a picture of him with his auburn hair looking especially spiky and gelled.

Two things were clear to Rose:

1. Lindsey Borzini wanted her brother's autograph; and
2. Lindsey Borzini was under the influence of magical baked goods.

Just before Lindsey reached Ty, the lumbering form of Mr. Borzini appeared out of nowhere like a defensive lineman and tackled his own daughter to the ground. The two of them lay there in a heap, wrestling on the brick floor of the plaza: Lindsey screaming and reaching desperately toward Ty, and Mr. Borzini pinning her by her shoulders and trying to avoid the wild waving of her fists.

"What has gotten into you, Lindzer Tart?" he cried.

All Lindsey could say in response was, "TY! Tyyyyyyyyy!"

Mr. Borzini look up at Ty while Lindsey whacked him in the side of the head. "She's been like this all morning. I don't know what's wrong with her. Maybe if you just say hi?"

Ty walked over and knelt down on one knee. Lindsey clawed at his jean-covered knee. "Um . . . hi," Ty whispered.

Lindsey's eyes went wide, a look of calm washed over her face, then her eyes closed and her head went limp in her father's arms.

"Fainted again," Mr. Borzini said. "That's the fifth time she fainted today—all because she heard your name or saw your picture."

Rose caught Ty in a proud smirk, and she smacked him lightly on the back of the head.

"I don't get it. I mean, you're a good-looking kid and all," said Mr. Borzini, "but you're not *that* good looking." Mr. Borzini picked Lindsey up in his arms and lumbered away.

Rose and Ty had both heard the frightened confusion in Mr. Borzini's voice. Rose didn't need to admonish her brother any further.

Ty turned to her and sighed. "I *know*, I know. We'll find a recipe to fix it."

Lily and Chip walked over with Sage and Leigh. "What was *that* all about?" Sage asked.

"It seems Ty has an ardent suitor!" Aunt Lily patted him on the shoulder and smiled. "It's not so surprising, darling. You look like a model, only a little shorter and younger. A miniature model!"

Ty's cheeks blushed a deep crimson.

"Hey!" Sage asked. "Does this have anything to do with what you guys were making yesterday when you tricked Lily and me into running after Leigh all day, and then the cookies you made last night after you told me to go to bed?" He put both hands on his hips like a stern mother.

Rose looked at the freckles on Sage's nose and thought that perhaps it was time to stop lying to her younger brother, who was clearly more perceptive than she gave him credit for.

"Did you trick me into chasing after Leigh yesterday?" Aunt Lily asked, her mouth a large O.

Ty gasped indignantly. "Of course not! Why would we do that to our favorite aunt?"

Rose then saw a way to keep Chip and Lily out of the house in order to fix the mess. "I have an idea! There is a big mess in the bakery, as we all know, and there is a lot of cake on the floor, and we just don't feel right leaving it like that."

"It looks like a cake bomb went off in there," Ty said.

"So why don't you two enjoy a relaxing French

lunch—with many courses, *multiple* courses—while we go and clean up the bakery?" Rose finished, trying not to look like the cat who caught the canary.

"Yes! Ty and Rose will clean up the bakery!" said Sage.

"You too, Sage!" Rose said, making sure to include Sage this time around. "The non-adults will clean up the bakery, for a change."

Lily and Chip looked at one another quizzically, then, after a moment, Aunt Lily shrugged and said, "All right! How kind! And now for Leigh's escargots!"

Leigh shook her head. "Uh-uh. Don't want 'em."

Lily pursed her lips and said, "Okay, but we are *still* having lunch. I've been looking for an opportunity to speak with Chip alone." She smiled devilishly.

Chip gulped as Lily slipped her arm into his, and together they strolled inside.

Sage was pouting. "Why do I have to clean the bakery too?" he whined.

Rose pulled Sage and Ty into a huddle. Leigh sidled in between Rose and Sage, sat on the ground in the middle of the huddle, and took off her shoes.

"This is classified intelligence, Sage," Rose said. "Can you keep this top secret?"

Sage stopped pouting and nodded with fervor. "I'll keep it the toppest secret."

That wasn't reassuring, but Rose pressed on. "We've been having some trouble with the *you-know-what*," she said. "We did a recipe, and it went wrong—"

Ty cut in. "Actually, it went *right*. But now we have to go back to the house to figure out how to reverse it."

"Exactly," Rose said. "So, your mission, should you choose to accept it—"

"You can count on me!" Sage said.

"—is to watch Leigh while Ty and I find a recipe to fix it!"

Rose smiled, glad that she'd found a way to make Sage feel included.

Sage angrily broke away. "Heck no! Babysitting is

not spy work. I want to be on the front lines. I want some action."

Leigh leaped up. "Me too!" she shouted. "Action!"

Ty grumbled, "Ahhh, fine."

"We don't have forever, so let's do this," Rose said. "And let's not make any mistakes this time."

As Rose and her siblings passed the sprawling green lawn of Calamity Falls Elementary School, she heard kids shouting like they were on a runaway carnival ride. Scattered across the wide expanse of the lawn, approximately two hundred children were engaged in what looked very much like a war.

Half of them had painted their faces yellow and patrolled the north end of the lawn, while the kids on the southern half had painted their faces blue. The blue-faced kids were hiding behind a half-dozen teacher's desks, which they had somehow dragged from the school building and lined up like a barricade. Stacked behind the desks were hundreds of supple blue water balloons.

"It's Wednesday," Rose whispered. "Why aren't they all in summer camp?"

Sage gulped. "Mr. Fanner is not going to be happy about this," he said solemnly. Rose and Ty had each gone through Calamity Falls Elementary School terrified of Mr. Fanner, who stormed through the halls every morning and handed out pink detention slips if he saw so much as an untied shoelace.

But then the strangest thing happened: All of the summer-camp teachers (minus Miss Thistle) made their way down the center of the lawn, smack through the middle of the balloon war, and none tried to stop it. All of them sauntered behind Principal Fanner, who wore a tweed jacket and spectacles and looked like an old-fashioned college professor.

He was smiling, which was something Rose had never seen Mr. Fanner do. Until that moment, she'd doubted that he even had teeth.

The teachers reached the sidewalk without getting hit by a stray balloon, then turned in the direction of the Bliss kids.

When Mr. Fanner spotted Rose and her brothers, his smile disappeared. He raised a finger and started wagging it. "Why are you not at the bakery?" he asked, irritated.

Rose took a deep breath. "Oh, we had some technical difficulties earlier today," she replied. "The bakery is closed until tomorrow."

The group of teachers standing behind Mr. Fanner let out a disappointed groan.

"Now what are we going to do?" shouted Ms. Spatz, Rose's third-grade teacher, a woman whose two front teeth overlapped.

Mr. Fanner pointed his finger right between Rose's eyes. "I closed summer camp early today because I didn't feel like teaching. I wanted cake. Badly. My friends want cake too. And you're telling us that we can't get any?"

Rose suddenly remembered Chip's list of people to whom he'd given free Cookies of Truth: "Miss Thistle, the teacher—all the teachers, actually."

So this was the truth about teachers: As badly as Rose sometimes wanted to leave school and eat a piece of cake, her teachers probably wanted to do the same thing, ten times worse.

"Fine," Mr. Fanner spat. "We shall go elsewhere. We shall drive to the Starbucks in Humbleton." Mr. Fanner turned his nose up at Rose and her brothers and marched away, the rest of the teachers following suit.

Sage turned to Rose and Ty, a mixture of wonder and horror on his face. "What did you *do?*"


When Rose and her siblings walked into the kitchen, they found Mrs. Carlson waiting for them, shaking her fist in the air. "Where have you children been?"

"You fell asleep, Mrs. Carlson, so we went to lunch," said Sage.

Mrs. Carlson squinted evilly at Sage. "Fair enough," she growled. "But I shan't let you out of my sight again. Your parents called, and I had to make up a lie that you were all taking a shower!"

"At the same time?" Ty asked.

"Well, that's where the lie fell apart, see? The point is, I'm not letting any of you out of my sight." She was shaking her fists so furiously that the rollers were coming out of her blond hair.

Rose said, "All right, well, why don't you watch Leigh outside while we clean up in here."

Mrs. Carlson nodded and ushered Leigh into the backyard, where she started pushing her on the swing. "Don't you dare photograph me, child!" Rose heard her shout.

Rose let out a tiny sigh of relief. When they were safely out of Mrs. Carlson's sight, they filed one by one into the walk-in fridge, Ty leading the way with the flashlight.

"Oh boy," Rose muttered to herself, closing the fridge door behind her.

Sage was rooting around on the wall near the eggs. He pulled out two cartons, just inches from the rolling-pin-shaped knob that opened the secret cellar.

"Put those back!" Rose barked, running over and replacing the cartons of eggs herself.

"What?" he shouted. "They're just eggs!"

Ty piped in. "Do what Rose says," he commanded.

Sage smiled at Rose. "Sorry," he said. Sage would do anything if Ty told him to—even if it meant respecting his older sister.

Rose winked at Ty and opened the door to the library, where the three huddled over the book on its wooden podium. Sage flipped the pages as Rose and Ty searched for something that could work as an antidote to madness, or a magical eraser.

"Here," said Ty. "This one."

Rose read the recipe aloud:

### *Sit-Down-and-Stop-Chattering Scones*

*Madam Hannah Bliss did make these scones in 1895 on the Lower East Side of Manhattan, where she was a schoolteacher. One year, her students were particularly unruly, so she fed them these scones and they were unable to utter a sound for the rest of the year. It was as if their lips fused together.*

*Nota Bene: Madam Hannah Bliss later regretted the making of these scones, as she was eventually prosecuted for causing mutism among an entire community of children.*

Ty nodded happily. "That'll get everyone to shut up, right?"

Rose shook her head. "No, Ty," she said. "We don't want to make people mute, we just want to reverse what we did. Turn everything upside down. . . ."

As she said the words, Rose turned to the very back of the book and found a series of smaller pages that sat nestled in a hollowed-out section of the back cover. The front page of this section was labeled ALBATROSS'S APOCRYPHA, and the paper was unlike that of the rest of the book, which was a creamy white. These pages were thinner and grayer and felt rough and crusty, like a cat's tongue. None of the recipes had dates or stories describing their origins. Rose thought it strange that this section should be labeled Albatross, when Lily had said that that was the name of her great-great-great-grandfather. Could it be the same Albatross?

She pulled the little gray booklet from its shallow cabinet in the back cover and flipped quickly through the pages. One recipe title caught her eye.

### *Turn-Around-Inside-Out-Upside-Down Cake*

"This is what we need," said Rose affirmatively. "Something that will just reverse everything."

Sage shook his head. "I don't know. . . . That one looks shady."

"Well, I'd rather have something that was a late addition to the book that's correct than something that's gonna sew everyone's lips together," Rose said.

Ty and Sage ultimately nodded in agreement, and Rose pulled out her notebook to make a copy.

When they emerged from the kitchen with the recipe for the cake, Mrs. Carlson was standing in the middle of the kitchen with Leigh.

"There is something wrong with the child," said Mrs. Carlson, her face even more twisted and confused than usual.

Then Rose saw what she was talking about.

"My family has a magical cookbook!" Leigh shouted from where she was sitting on the floor. "They keep it in the fridge! Rose has the key! My family has a magical cookbook! They keep it in the fridge! Rose has the key!"

Rose's eyes darted over to the plate of extra Cookies of Truth, which was now empty except for a few sad crumbs.

"Did Leigh eat those cookies?" Rose asked.

"I suppose she did!" said Mrs. Carlson. "I brung

her in here so that I could use the powder room, and she snuck an entire platter of cookies into her gullet! You leave a child alone for five minutes and she gets herself in trouble!"

"My family has a magical cookbook!" Leigh shouted.

"Leigh, stop it! Keep your mouth shut!" Ty shouted. But Leigh couldn't control herself. She just kept shouting the same thing over and over.

"Why is she spouting nonsense about a magical cookbook?" Mrs. Carlson asked.

"I have no idea. She's always had a very advanced imagination," Rose said, panicking about her little sister. If Aunt Lily came home, she was going to hear everything.

Just as Rose was thinking about a possible solution, a tidal wave of screaming rose like a tsunami outside the bakery.

"What is that godforsaken shrieking?" Mrs. Carlson asked.

Rose looked up and saw twenty or so girls clawing at the door, banging at the windows, pressing their lips against the glass and waving at Rose and her brothers. And there were more behind those. Almost all of them were holding a copy of the Calamity Falls Middle School yearbook in one hand and a pen in the other.

"Ty," Rose said. "You said it was a few girls."

Ty gave Rose an aw-shucks kind of look. "A few . . . dozen?"

## CHAPTER II

# Recipe the Third: Turn-Around-Inside-Out-Upside-Down Cake

*T*he sound of banging made Rose look back in horror.

Out the backdoor, six rabid girls had pressed their flushed faces to the glass. More girls bounced on the trampoline, trying to get a look into the kitchen over the heads of the others. A girl stood on each of the swings—even the baby swing—and one brave girl had climbed on top of the rusty barbecue grate, ignoring the bits of burned hamburger stuck to the grill. Their eyes were bulging out of their heads, big as Ping-Pong balls.

This was scary stuff.

Ty pushed a spike of gelled hair off his face, and the girls let out a collective wail.

"What are these ridiculous girls screaming about?" Mrs. Carlson asked.

Rose already knew the answer as she eased through the dark brown oak saloon doors into the front room.

At the sight of her, the dozens of girls who'd congregated outside the front of the shop let loose a deafening roar of disappointment that rattled the glass front of the display case. *"Boooooooooooo!"*

"Go away!" Rose shouted. "Ty doesn't like you!" But she could barely hear herself above the din.

Then a singular voice rose from the back of the crowd. "If he doesn't come out now, I will rip someone's face off!" One girl, taller and stronger than all the others, was hurtling toward the front of the crowd, throwing shorter girls to the ground as she passed them. That girl was Ashley Knob.

Her long hair had been curled into fancy ring-lets so shiny and so blond that you had to squint to look at them directly. Her lip gloss shimmered like an expensive watch. Slung over one shoulder was a bag from which a frightened Chihuahua looked out, clearly wishing he were somewhere else. A ring of space opened up around her. Even in the depths of a spell, the girls of Calamity Falls always knew to make way for Ashley Knob.

Ashley screamed, banging on the window with her fists. "I will set all the furniture from my daddy's store on fire and throw it through this window!"

The other girls followed suit and pounded on the glass with their fists. Fearing that the window would give way, Rose thought it best to give the girls what they wanted. "Okay, okay! I'll hand him over! Just stop it!"

Ashley Knob raised her arm high, and instantly the banging and chanting stopped.

Rose found Ty in the kitchen, curled up behind the chopping block with the collar of his button-down shirt pulled up over his eyes.

"They want to see you," Rose said.

"This is ludicrous!" said Mrs. Carlson. "These girls ought to be ashamed of themselves!"

Rose watched as Mrs. Carlson charged through the saloon doors, then eased herself through the front door of the bakery, taking care not to let in any of the rabid teenagers. "You are all acting like a bunch of ninnies! You need to go home to your parents, now!"

Ashley Knob seized Mrs. Carlson by the rollers in her hair as the mob lifted her up over their heads and pushed her to the back of the crowd. She tried desperately to claw her way back to the front door, but the girls were too strong. Mrs. Carlson disappeared.

Rose yanked Ty up by his spiky hair. "You need to get in the front, now! They have Mrs. Carlson! Who knows what they'll do to her!"

Ty cowered out of sight of the window. "No way. I

don't even like her."

Rose shoved him. "You *have* to go out there and calm them down."

"How am I supposed to do that?"

It was a good question. But Rose thought of Devin and immediately knew the answer: "You have to kiss the ringleader. Ashley Knob."

"That prissy, self-important brat? I'd rather kiss Mrs. Carlson!"

"I can arrange that," Rose said.

Ty fell to his knees. "Please, Rose! If I put my mouth anywhere near those glittery, bubble-gum-gloss-covered fish lips, my life at school will be ruined. She'll keep me trapped in her talons like she keeps that poor dog trapped in her purse. Do you want me to be a dog in a purse, Rose? Is that really what you want?"

Rose rolled her eyes. "You don't have to *actually* kiss her. You just have to get her to faint, so she doesn't break the window. It'll be easy."

* * *

Rose pulled Sage and Leigh into the front room, and the three stood behind the counter and watched as Ty pushed through the saloon doors. The girls screamed like they had just seen Elvis. Or Justin Bieber.

"This is better than when Daddy bought me a helicopter for my sweet sixteen!" Ashley Knob screamed. "And I *looooooove* helicopters!"

"Here goes nothing," Ty muttered over his shoulder. He produced a toy megaphone that Albert kept in the kitchen cabinets and pressed its bullhorn against the tiny mail slot in the glass next to the front door.

"Ashley Knob." Ty was on his knees, speaking timidly into the megaphone.

"Speak, my most delicious one!"

"Um, kiss me. Like, through the glass," he stammered.

"I die!" Ashley cried, then pressed her shimmering pink lips to the glass in a mushy pucker. Ty nervously pressed his lips to the glass where Ashley's expectant mouth quivered on the other side.

Sage made a retching sound, and Leigh giggled. "My family has a magical cookbook!" she said, snapping a picture of the screaming mob.

"It's working!" Rose shouted to her older brother. "Look!" As soon as Ty put his lips to the glass, Ashley had fallen into a deep trance and sunk to the ground. "Now do it to the other ones!"

"Do I have to fake kiss everyone?" Ty asked, obviously upset by the prospect.

"No, just, like, say nice things to them. They'll be so overwhelmed that they'll totally pass out." Rose tried very hard to hide the fact that she was enjoying this just the tiniest bit. She had never seen her big brother so terrified before. He was usually the one in control, too busy to bother with anything having to do with the bakery. Or with Rose. Now he was turning to *her* for advice.

"Nice things?" Ty complained. "Just look at them. Do you really think these girls deserve compliments?"

"There's no time for thinking, Ty!" Rose shouted.

"Just *doing*! Go forth and compliment!"

"Callie," Ty called. A girl with brown pigtails stepped up to the window. "Your hair is bouncy." Callie's eyes rolled back in her head and she wilted in ecstasy.

"Jenna," he called as another girl with braces and round glasses approached. "You have glasses and braces." Jenna stiffened like a tree and fell to the ground.

"Lisa." A girl wearing what to Rose looked like a potato sack approached. "Lisa. You're . . . alive." Lisa spun in a joyful circle before falling to her knees and swooning.

Rose watched what was happening like she watched scary movies: with her fingers in front of her face. "Promise me you'll never act this way over *anyone*, Leigh," Rose said, squeezing her little sister's puffy cheeks.

Ty called the girls out one by one, doling out the most lackluster compliments Rose had ever heard—but they worked every time. By the time he was done, there were only ten or so girls left standing. "Don't stop now!"

"I don't even know their names!" Ty moaned.

"Well, then try singing something," she said, sharing a private smile with Sage.

"I am *not* singing."

"Ty, we're in the home stretch. We can't have these girls busting in on us while we're trying to bake."

"But I don't know any songs."

"Just sing anything."

Ty grumbled and stuck the megaphone against the mail slot.

*"Jingle bells, Batman smells . . ."*

Ty began timidly. The remaining ten girls surged against the glass and dropped one by one to the ground.

*"Robin laid an egg . . ."*

Ty abandoned the megaphone and danced freestyle around the bakery, humming and jumping long after the last of the girls had expired.

When Ty finally realized that he no longer needed to sing and dance, he stiffened and cleared his throat and straightened his shirt. The curb outside the bakery was strewn with unconscious girls.

"You did great, Ty. That oughtta hold 'em for a little while," Rose said, stifling a giggle.

"All in a hard day's work," Ty said, glancing over at Sage, who was copying Ty's dance moves by himself in the corner.

Mrs. Carlson clambered through the piles of young ladies and tore open the front door. "Well, I never!" was all she could say. She wrapped her arms around herself and shook from the trauma.

"Mrs. Carlson, why don't you stay in here and stand guard with Leigh? Ty and Sage and I are going to make the girls some cake so they'll go away," Rose suggested.

"Do you really think these crazed creatures with their crazed teenage hormones are going to be quelled by a bit of plain old *cake*?!" she hollered.

"This is special cake," said Rose.

Leigh perked up. "My family has a magical cookbook!"

Mrs. Carlson scowled and pulled Leigh onto her lap. "Make it snappy, then."

Rose, Ty, and Sage gathered around the kitchen chopping block and consulted their copy of the recipe for Turn-Around-Inside-Out-Upside-Down Cake. Rose glanced at the clock. "Lily and Chip should be a couple of hours at lunch."

Ty rolled up his sleeves and smirked. "At Pierre Guillaume's? A couple of hours if they eat *fast*. That place has the worst service of any restaurant in history."

The list of ingredients was fairly standard—milk, flour, eggs, sugar, butter, baking powder, salt, strawberries—except for the last ingredient, which was this:

## the Tears of a Warlock*†

Rose had made sure to copy the note about the tears, having learned her lesson about the importance of asterisks.

*A warlock's eye does not produce tears of sadness, because a warlock has no deep feeling. When a warlock cries, it is a freakish reversal, a catastrophic event. This provides the needed reversal for the recipe.
†This recipe will begin to work immediately but will reach its maximum potential after twelve hours.

Rose looked at Ty. "Why don't you go get the warlock's eye?"

Ty shook his head violently. "Get it yourself. I've already cried enough tears today—did you see the way Ashley Knob licked the window? That's going to haunt me for the rest of my life."

"Fine. I'll go. In the meantime, you and Sage better close the shutters on the windows. We don't want anyone seeing what we're doing in here."

Rose was relieved to find that all the jars were exactly as they'd left them: The first wind of autumn was still turning behind its blue glass, the Dwarf of Perpetual Sleep was still slumbering, and the warlock's eye was still . . . floating in yellowish juice. She reached for it and was about to close her hands around the jar when she noticed something: There was a breeze in the cellar.

The air seemed to breathe in and out, and at first she thought she was just imagining something, but then she noticed that the cool gray mist that hung on the floor was moving: It gently wafted forward and then back, again and again. Was there an air vent in the secret pantry that she hadn't noticed before?

Rose tiptoed around the shelf, the blueish light from the jars making everything look like it was underwater, and looked for the source of the mist. There were no vents in the walls—just shelf after shelf of jars. Whatever it was had to be on the floor.

At last she slowly sank to her knees and crawled.

On the floor, in the corner of the cellar, was a rusted iron grate like the ones in the house the heat came from. Only this one wasn't warm; it was cold to the touch, and the mist was bubbling up from beneath it.

Rose leaned forward and pressed her ear against it. A sound of air being drawn into something wet and huge, then blown out: breathing. Something was under the house.

Goose bumps rippled across her arms and neck, and Rose slowly began backing away from the grate. As she did, the whisk-shaped key on its string slipped forward out of her shirt and softly clanged against the metal.

The breathing stopped. And then a voice she barely heard but more sensed as a vibration in her bones said, *Who is THERE?*

Rose held her breath.

*I HEAR you,* the voice said. *I SMELL you.*

Rose closed her eyes and tried to breathe quietly through her open mouth.

A prettier girl—or a more powerful and important one—wouldn't be stuck in this kind of situation, on her hands and knees in a magical cellar with some terrifying *thing* awoken and ready to do God knew what.

*And I KNOW you,* the voice said. *Help me, and I can help you win your heart's desire. Is it fortune and fame that you seek? Is it beauty that you crave? Then find the ingredient labeled Tincture of Venus. Mix it with the right recipe, and you will outshine Helen of Troy. Even your aunt Lily! Just try a pinch in your tea.*

By now Rose had backed up against the foot of the steps, and she could no longer make out the iron bars of the grate. Whatever it was under the cellar, it somehow knew about Aunt Lily, and about Rose's deepest desires.

She silently stood up and grabbed the warlock's eye.

Rose took the jar and behind it caught a glimpse of another jar, this one empty except for a clamshell compact that glowed around its edges. The words "TINCTURE OF VENUS" were printed on the label in little gold letters.

What she wouldn't give to be pretty like Aunt Lily—to have power in her fingertips, to be important, to be able to make anyone do anything that she wanted. Girls went crazy over Ty because he was handsome. What if Rose were gorgeous? Would the boys in school go gaga over her? Probably.

Rose lost herself for a moment, imagining what it would be like to stroll down the middle-school halls and make heads turn. Kids would clamor after her, wanting to be friends with her instead of calling her things like Shake 'N Bake.

The other kids at school—and the teachers, too!—would dote on her every word, take everything she said more seriously. And maybe her brothers would start being nicer to her. And maybe her parents would trust her more too, and let her bake things from the Cookery Booke, and teach her the right way to do it. Or maybe, once she was pretty, she wouldn't even need the bakery. She could leave Calamity Falls, go out and conquer the world—

"Rose! Come *on*!" she heard Ty shout from the kitchen.

Her brothers. They needed her.

Rose glanced back at the Tincture of Venus, back at the mist that had spoken to her. "No, thanks," she whispered, and climbed up the steps out of the cellar, warlock's eye in hand. "Not now."

Rose emerged from the fridge just as Ty and Sage finished dumping sacks of flour and teaspoon after teaspoon of baking powder into the stand mixer's huge metal vat.

"Here's enough for forty-four cakes," Sage announced. "We figured we have to make enough slices for everyone in town, which is about twenty-two hundred people, so, if there are fifty really thin slices per cake, then forty-four should do it. . . ." He held up a cake-cutting diagram he'd made.

"Great work, Sage." Rose laid the barbed-wire-wrapped mason jar on the counter, and the eye bobbed up and down in its yellowed preservative juice. It had an iris the color of lavender and a knobby blue tail—Rose knew this was the optic nerve, the bundle of cords that connected it to the brain. It was both beautiful and hideous at the same time.

Sage flinched when he saw the pickled eye. "Ugh! What is *that*?" He quivered as he picked up the jar. The eye rolled around and opened, staring straight at Sage in the dim light of the covered kitchen windows. "Where did you get this thing?"

Rose took the jar from him before he dropped it. She wanted to tell Ty about the voice, but not in front of Sage. "Give me that."

"Mom and Dad have some more . . . exotic stuff," said Ty. "In a secret pantry. We'll show you later."

"Now," said Rose, "the real question is, how do we get this ugly thing to cry?"

Ty folded one arm over his chest and rubbed his chin with the other. "Hmm," he said. "Well, I think we should start by taking it out of the jar and holding it over the batter, so we're ready to collect the tears."

"Good idea," Rose said, and slid the jar to Ty.

"Oh, no—I'm not touching that," said Ty, clearly grossed out.

"You always say you want to be more involved, Sage," Rose said, pushing the jar toward her little brother. "Here's your chance."

Sage just shrieked and threw his arms in front of his freckled, chubby cheeks.

"Fine!" Rose scowled and bent back the barbwire, then unlocked the metal clasp of the mason jar.

When she opened the lid, the smell was indescribable. It was like water in a vase of rotten daisies. It was like vinegar that had been used to bathe a sick frog. It was like yogurt from the Middle Ages. It was like the sweat of a corpse, if corpses could sweat.

"Who *farted*?" Sage cried.

Rose clamped her nose with one hand and grabbed at the trailing optic nerve with the other. It flapped away like a fish in a pet store that doesn't want to be caught, but after a few tries, she had looped the bundle of nerves around her finger and pulled the dangling eye from the jar.

Ty and Sage were both holding their noses and gagging.

"How are we going to get it to cry?" Ty groaned.

"Beats me," Rose wondered aloud. "What would you say to someone to make them cry?"

Sage stood over the dangling eye. "Your dog just died!" he shouted.

The eye turned itself around and glared at Sage, as if to say, *Nice try.*

Ty grumbled, "You are the ugliest thing I've ever seen!"

The eyelid squinted itself shut in such a way that it almost seemed to be smiling.

"Dude, you just complimented it!" Sage said.

Rose furrowed her brow. How could you get someone—or a severed part of someone, with no feelings—to cry? Rose glanced over at the shuttered windows, where the gaggle of girls was beginning to stir.

Then she knew what to do.

"Ty! Hold this!" she cried, thrusting the eye into Ty's unsuspecting hand. He shrieked like a baby as he clenched his fingers around the stringy, slimy nerves.

Rose ran to the pantry and grabbed a cleaver and an onion, the biggest yellow onion she could find. She brought them over to where Ty was dangling the eye over the mixing vat. She sliced right down the middle of the onion, cleaving it in half. Then she hacked those halves in half, and kept hacking until the board was covered in little white cubes.

And as she chopped the onion, the spicy, earthen smell of onion crept up Rose's nose and made her eyes sting so badly that she could barely breathe. So she did what came naturally: She cried. She cried because of the thing in the cellar, because it was telling the truth—she wanted more than anything to be important, to be famous, to matter. To be pretty.

She sniffled and waved the cutting board full of onions under the warlock's eye.

Ty and Sage had both buried their eyes in their elbows, so only Rose saw when the eye blinked angrily and let drop one thick, oily black tear, which plopped into the vat, and then another, and then another, until gobs of black were oozing out of the corners of the disembodied eye.

"You guys," Rose whispered. "Look!"

The eye itself began to glow with a cold purple light, and the black tears that had seeped into the batter sizzled and popped. Suddenly, the enormous bowl began to spin round on its axis, with a slow metal rattling at first, then faster and faster, like the sort of carnival ride that always made Rose throw up.

The three of them stepped back. "I'm getting a bad feeling," Sage said.

"Shhh," Ty said.

The batter was whipped to the walls of the vat, then

crept up the sides and bubbled over. But it didn't spill to the floor. Instead, while the vat kept spinning, the batter kept rising until it was floating near the ceiling in a fat gloopy ball. The shapeless dough rearranged itself into a human face with giant furrowed brows and deep, hollow eyes that glared at Rose. A mouth formed beneath those and wordlessly shouted at her.

"Leave me alone!" she cried.

Then the eye stopped glowing, its eyelids closing with an almost audible snap. The face dissolved into the rest of the batter, and whole thing dropped *splat* back into the vat.

It was over.

Ty dropped the eye back into the jar. Rose clasped the lid on tight and took it back to the secret pantry. As she slid it back into place on the shelf, she could swear she heard it—or something—grumble.

Sage, Rose, and Ty filled up every available cake pan with the batter, which had turned a sickly looking gray-pink color, and crammed them into all the ovens, which they had turned on full blast—the four stacking wall ovens, and the beehive-shaped cast-iron stove in the corner. It was as hot as the basement of a coal-powered steamboat.

After forty minutes, the little red kitchen timer that Purdy used for her cakes made an optimistic little *Ping!* sound, and the three Bliss kids flew into action. Ty and Sage pulled all the cakes out to cool, while Rose began slicing the cake and laying individual portions onto paper plates with a plastic fork stuck in each one.

The three worked in feverish silence. No one said a word until all of the cake was sliced and plated. Every surface in the kitchen was covered with slices of magical dessert.

By this time, most of the girls had awakened, and Rose could hear them listlessly banging on the window again in the front.

Rose loaded two dozen plates onto a massive tray the size of a card table, and she and Sage ferried it to the front room. They set the tray down near the door and rapped on the window.

"Hurry!" said Mrs. Carlson, who'd been watching Leigh the whole time the kids prepared their magical dough. "The beasts have come to!"

"Silence!" Rose shouted. Aunt Lily and Chip could return at any moment—she had to work fast.

Only the girls didn't stop screaming and banging on the window. They only banged harder. Rose felt completely invisible.

Then Ty swept in and yelled through the megaphone again, *"Be quiet!"*

At the sound of his voice, the girls went completely silent and stood at attention.

"Because I love you all so much, I made you some cake!" he shouted, holding up a piece. This was met with a collective sigh. "If you want any, you have to form a line by the door! Single file!"

"It's as if women's lib was all but a dream!" Mrs. Carlson muttered.

The girls scrambled to line up, clawing at one another to be closest to the door. With trembling hands, Rose unlocked the door, visions dancing through her head of being trampled by a sneering mob of mean girls.

"If you eat your *whole* piece of cake," Ty explained, overenunciating like he was talking to a roomful of kindergarteners, "then I will personally . . . give you a hug and sign your yearbook with my name."

"Just your name?" one of the girls screeched, her voice sharp and piercing.

Ty shrugged. "Um, and a smiley face."

"OMG! OMG! OMG!" the girl shouted, and others began to join in as well.

Rose opened the door six inches—just enough to pass the paper plates through. As she handed slice after slice to the girls, they stared right through her at Ty.

Ashley Knob was the last to take a slice of cake. Her blond ringlets were now a wild mess of frizz and dirt. Rose thrust a fork at her, but she just scooped the slice into her manicured hands and gobbled it down whole.

Ashley's eyes widened. She turned around without saying anything, then marched away slowly and deliberately. In her wake, all the girls threw their plates on the ground and walked away.

"What sort of cake is that?" said Mrs. Carlson. "It doesn't seem like they actually liked it very much. I wouldn't put that gray stuff in my mouth."

Rose sighed. Mrs. Carlson was right. Even though they'd devoured it, they hadn't seemed to enjoy it.

"Did that seem right to you?" whispered Ty, his lean, tan arms crossed in front of his dress shirt.

Rose wasn't sure. It was odd, the way they'd just dangled their arms, spun around, and walked away like robots, but isn't that what they'd wanted them to do? Go away? Besides, the recipe wouldn't reach its maximum potential for another twelve hours, which meant tomorrow morning.

Leigh was sitting in the middle of the filthy bakery floor expectantly with her arms raised in the air, like she was asking for a hug. Or cake.

"My family has a magical cookbook!" she yelled. "They keep it in the back of the fridge! Rose has the key!"

Rose handed her sister a slice of the fluffy gray-pink stuff, and Leigh scarfed it down in two big, messy bites.

She promptly stopped talking. She also promptly stopped looking Rose in the eye. She just stared past Rose.

"Leigh? You okay?" Rose said.

Leigh nodded, still staring into the distance, then crawled slowly into the kitchen and up the stairs to her bedroom.

"Where is she going?" Sage asked.

Rose followed her upstairs and watched as Leigh crawled into her bed, turned on her glowing ladybug night-light, and pulled the covers under her chin. She lay there, silent, and closed her eyes.

"Are you okay?" Rose asked again. "Leigh?"

But Leigh was already snoring. It was very much unlike Leigh to go to bed in the middle of the day, without any supper. But then again, she *had* just eaten a whole slice of cake.

In the hallway, Rose passed Mrs. Carlson, who announced, "Since the young one is napping, I'm going to take a nap as well. There's been too much action for the day, and my blood pressure can't take it. The muscleman and the supermodel ought to be back soon, anyway. They can take care of that mess downstairs," she said. "You are a strange family. You know that, don't you?"

Rose nodded, and Mrs. Carlson said no more, just lumbered slowly away.

Outside in the backyard, Ty and Sage were stacking the plates of cake in the little red wagon that Albert kept in the garage. Rose remembered when her father used to cart her and Ty around town on errands. Now Ty was using it to cart around magical cake that their parents would surely disapprove of.

"I don't know about this," Rose said. "Leigh is acting weird. She went to sleep."

"Good," Ty said. "That oughtta keep her out of our hair."

"But isn't that a bit weird?" A dull ache had settled in Rose's gut, and that usually meant that she needed to stop whatever she was doing and reevaluate it. The cake had made the girls walk away like robots, and Leigh just fell right to sleep. Was that healthy? It didn't look like the other recipes in the book, and it contained black oily tears from a warlock. Was this really the right solution? She wished she could call her parents and ask. But, of course, she couldn't.

"We didn't do all this baking for nothing," Ty huffed. "I am personally making sure that everyone in town eats a piece of this stupid cake." Ty folded his arms over his chest. "Rose, we have to fix the town before Mom and Dad get back."

"Oh . . . you're right," Rose said optimistically. She didn't want Ty to think that she was weak. "It'll definitely work."

Ty pulled a map of Calamity Falls out of his pocket

and walked away, pulling the cart with one hand. "This should take, oh . . . seventeen hours," he said grumpily, and he pulled the wagon out the driveway and down the street, leaving Rose and Sage standing alone in the backyard. They stepped back into the kitchen and exhaled.

Now there was just the matter of the mess.

Not only had they failed to clean the front room of the bakery after the librarians' brawl, but they also had dirtied the kitchen beyond repair. Forty-four filthy cake pans were stacked in teetering piles in the kitchen sink; dried gobs of gray-pink dough clung to the sides of the mixing vat and also to the wall and cabinet doors; and Rose had no idea what the clear puddles on the floor were—water, egg white, sweat, or warlock's eye preservative liquid.

Not to mention the mess Rose and Sage found when they wandered outside: Dozens of little dirty paper plates and plastic forks littered the sidewalk. The seething horde of girls had trampled all of the flowers and shrubs outside the house, and there was a gaping hole in the middle of the beloved trampoline where one girl had jumped too high and fallen straight through.

When they opened the door to go back into the kitchen, Chip and Aunt Lily were back from their lunch at Pierre Guillaume's, looking, indeed, like a supermodel and a muscleman.

"I thought you said you were going to *clean up*!" Chip shouted. He stormed angrily upstairs to fetch cleaning supplies. "Honestly, Rose! What were you thinking?"

Lily cornered Rose and Sage by the walk-in refrigerator. She batted her eyelashes in a way that was both attractive and terrifying. "Would either of you mind very much telling me just what is going on?"

Before Rose could think of a suitable lie, Sage blurted out, "It's all because of the cookbook!"

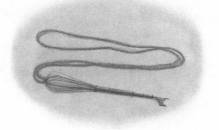

## CHAPTER 12:
# Lying to Aunt Lily

"Coooook-booooook?" Lily asked, drawing out the word to three times its usual length.

"Yes, um, the Betty Crocker cookbook!" Rose could barely breathe—she felt like the air was sticky maple syrup running down her nose and filling her lungs. "See, we made all this wonderful cake, and everyone came to have a piece, and that's why the yard is all trampled and there are all those plates on the lawn."

Lily knelt down, took off her beret, and shook her hair out—not that there was much hair to shake out. Rose noticed that Lily had a way of kneeling down whenever she wanted to say something important, so that her eyes were directly across from Rose's instead of three feet higher.

"What *kind* of cake did you make?" Lily asked, squinting in a way that let Rose know that Aunt Lily knew she was lying.

"Strawberry," said Rose without a moment's hesitation.

"Tell her what we really made!" Sage shouted.

Then Rose did something she wasn't proud of: She opened the walk-in refrigerator and shoved Sage inside.

She leaned up against the shut door to keep him from escaping, even as he screamed for mercy. It was a good thing she'd worn rubber-soled sneakers that morning, because she was able to hold the door shut just by bending her knees and wedging her sneakers against the floor.

Now his shouts were muffled. Rose knew that he was screaming about the cookbook, but he could just as easily have been screaming about wanting a Nintendo Wii.

"Regular old strawberry cake, eh?" said Lily, arching her perfect eyebrows. "Did Sage help?"

"Mmm-hmm!" Rose said, nodding. The fridge jolted against her back; Sage had begun throwing his entire body against the door.

"Rose," said Lily. "It's obvious that you're hiding something. You literally just locked your brother in the refrigerator. Why don't you just tell me what's really going on? It can't be *that* bad. Besides, I did tons of bad things when I was young. Once, I glued my father's shoes to the floor!" Lily let out a chuckle. "Can you believe that? Shoes! Glue! I mean, what was I thinking?"

At that moment, Rose was knocked to her knees as Sage burst triumphantly from the fridge. "I got a running start!" he crowed. "I'm strong!"

"There's no denying *that*," said Aunt Lily.

Then Sage remembered why he'd been pushed into the fridge in the first place. "Rose is lying!" he shouted, throwing his arms around Aunt Lily's long neck. "We made a cake from the *real* cookbook!"

"What cookbook?" Lily asked.

"We have a magical family cookbook," Sage said. "Our parents told us not to touch it, but we convinced Rose to let us."

Rose wiped off her knees and stood. She wanted badly to run to the phone and dial her mother and say, "Mama, we broke out the cookbook and almost wrecked the town and now Sage is telling our pretty, fake aunt about it"—but her tongue had gone all heavy and limp, like a wet sock, and she couldn't get it to move, much less form words.

Rose found this just the least bit strange, so she did a mini experiment. She forgot about Aunt Lily as she tried to remember how to count to ten in Latin. *"Unus. Duo. Tres,"* she muttered. *"Quattuor. Cinque.*

*Quinque?"* Was it with a *C* or a *Q*? Was *C* the Italian version? Rose's tongue had regained full function.

*I want to tell Mom about Aunt Lily,* Rose thought, and tried to say something out loud.

Her tongue went limp again.

So Rose wasn't imagining it—her tongue failed to function every time she thought about telling her mother about Aunt Lily. Certainly it was no accident—but there was no time to think about it now, because Sage was still folded in Lily's long arms, spilling bean after bean, like a broken sack of lentils being dragged along the sidewalk.

"I see," said Lily. "And where is this magical cookbook?"

"Behind the *tapestry* at the end of the walk-in *fridge*," Sage said, proudly patting his belly.

"Innnterrressstingg!" Lily cooed, drawing the word out into the length of an entire sentence. Lily turned to Rose and beckoned to her. Her face was filled with so much love, so much compassion, that Rose found herself inching over without even thinking about it. Lily held out her luxurious, soft hand with its long, polished fingers, and Rose slid her own grubby hand into it.

"Rose," said Lily. "I know you were lying to protect your parents. But if this cookbook got you into some trouble, it's important that you tell an adult about it," Lily said. "An adult in your family, one with a ladle on her back."

Rose steeled herself. She had handled the horde of screaming girls, and she could handle Aunt Lily. "We took care of it."

"How?"

"With cake." And that was it. Rose didn't need this mysterious stranger's help.

Lily smiled widely. "Fair enough, darling." Then the smile disappeared. "But I think you should give me the key to the storeroom—just in case any more nonadults should be tempted to break out the book and get into even *more* trouble."

The uncomfortable ache in Rose's stomach turned to full-on spasms at the thought of giving Lily the key. "I can't give you the key," said Rose. "Mom and Dad left it to me. But I promise that no one will touch the book again this week."

"Now, Rose," said Lily, showing all her teeth again in a way that should have been reassuring but wasn't, "isn't that what you promised your parents originally? And didn't you break out the cookbook anyway?"

The words stung. It was true. Perhaps Rose wasn't fit to be a magical baker. Or even a good daughter. Or even much of a girl. Rose tasted a single salty tear run into the corner of her mouth.

Sage lifted one finger high into the air and exclaimed, "*I* will hold the key!"

"What?" Rose groaned, twisting her blue dress with her fingers. "No way, Sage. You are by far the least responsible person in this family."

Now it was Sage's turn to cry. "No one *ever* lets me do *any*thing!" he screamed.

Lily brushed Rose's bangs away from her eyes and whispered, "Rose. I think you should let him hold the key. He wants to be taken seriously. If you don't start trusting him now, he's going to get the message that he's just a joke. And then he'll never take responsibility for anything."

Rose looked over at Sage, who could improvise a Shakespearean monologue better than anyone she knew, who could make anyone laugh, just by looking at them, and who loved Ty to distraction, if not quite Rose herself. Then she remembered how frustrated she felt when her parents didn't allow her any responsibility in the bakery, how insignificant. She didn't want to be the one to make Sage feel the same way. He was her brother, and he deserved a chance.

Rose went over to Sage, who'd begun maniacally jumping up and down and shouting. She tried to touch his shoulder to calm him, but he only jumped away.

"Okay, okay!" Rose shouted. "You can hold the key!"

Sage immediately stopped jumping and turned to her, panting, his tongue hanging slightly out of his mouth. He wore a look of suspicion. *"Why?"* he said, testing her.

"Because . . . I want you to be an actor one day," she said.

Sage crinkled up his nose like he smelled a dead rat. "You want me to be an *actor*?"

"Yes. Or a politician. Or something where you get to talk a lot. So I am letting you take responsibility by holding the key for a few days. But you are not to let anybody else *touch* it. And I mean *ANYBODY*," Rose said, cocking her head to indicate Aunt Lily, who was standing by the saloon doors with her hands delicately cupping her cheeks, looking very pleased.

Rose gently pulled the string around her neck up over her hair and placed it over Sage's puffy red head, like she was knighting him.

For the first time in ages, Sage wrapped his arms around Rose and hugged her. He hugged her so tightly that she had to pry him off just so she could breathe, but still—it made her smile.

Rose spent the rest of the afternoon washing cake pans in the kitchen while Lily and Chip cleaned up the front room, and Sage and a half-asleep Mrs. Carlson picked up the paper plates and plastic forks that dotted every inch of the ground within a hundred-yard radius.

Ty came home at around ten p.m. His collared shirt was soaking wet, his face was smeared with dirt and dust, and his hands were covered in blisters from pulling the wagon.

Rose poured him a glass of water. "Did you do it?" she asked.

Ty's eyes were already closed, and he drank down the full glass. He could only nod.

"*Everyone* in town ate a slice of cake?" she asked.

Ty nodded again. "So many people . . . ," he mumbled.

"Listen," Rose said. "I have to tell you what

happened. Sage spilled the beans to Aunt Lily about
the cookbook, and she wanted the key to the door,
but I gave it to Sage instead because it just didn't seem
right to give her the key."

Ty stumbled toward the stairs, Rose following.
"Are you listening, Ty?" she asked. But he just staggered up into the dark of the second story.

When they reached Sage and Ty's room and
creaked the door open, they saw a tall shadowy figure
sitting on Sage's bed.

It was Aunt Lily. Sage was asleep, and Lily was sitting near his shoulders, patting his hair.

"What are you doing up here?" Rose whispered.

Lily jumped up and spun around. She exhaled
loudly. "You frightened me!" she whispered, catching
her breath. "I was just . . . saying good night to Sage."
Then she slipped between Rose and Ty and sauntered
downstairs.

Rose breathed a sigh of relief when she saw the
little silver whisk lying on Sage's chest, glinting in the

moonlight, right where it was supposed to be.

Ty sank into his bed. Rose turned to leave, but then he reached up and grabbed her hand. "Hey, Rosita," he said. "That was actually kind of fun today."

Rose smiled wide.

"Minus the singing and the hours of toting cake around in a red wagon in the middle of July." He yawned. "Still, like, well done."

Rose wanted to say so much to him, and had Ty not been falling asleep, she might have. Something like, *Thank you so much for saying that because it means a lot to me today that we worked so well together because sometimes it can seem like you don't care about me at all because you're too busy being handsome and popular and I'm just your flour-covered kid sister who bugs you all the time but I love you more than I know how to say so I'm just glad you think I'm good at something.*

But all she said was "Good night, Ty."

And then she closed her brothers' door and went to the bathroom to wash the considerable grime from her face.

Then the portable phone rang and Rose answered, shutting the bathroom door behind her. It was her mother.

"I hope it's not too late, honey, but we just got back to our hotel!" said Purdy. "I had to check in on my kiddles! Did everything go smoothly today?"

Rose answered with a resounding "Yes!" because it *had* gone smoothly, in its own way. Sure, the town had been thrown into chaos, but she had fixed it, with her brothers' help. Rose felt guilty for not telling her mother the whole truth, but knew that someday she would take her mother out to tea and recount every detail, and Purdy would squeeze Rose to her chest and say, *That's my little baker!*

"Also," said Rose, "it might be too early to call it, but I think that me and Ty and Sage might be friends now."

Purdy laughed. "That's wonderful, sweetheart. What happened?"

Rose puzzled a minute. Was it that Ty and Sage both just wanted to learn magic in order to get closer to Aunt Lily? Or were they starting to like their sister?

She supposed it didn't really matter.

"I guess it's just that baking is really bringing us together."

"Well, that's what makes baking so magical, Rose."

Rose smirked to herself. *That, and all the stuff you keep in the secret pantry.*

"Good night, sweetheart."

"Good night, Mama."

Outside, the sky had grown dark and the first star had appeared. It glowed bigger and brighter and a little bit pinker than a star. *Maybe it's a planet*, Rose thought. *Maybe it's Mars.* Mars was Rose's favorite planet. It was named after the Roman god of war, and Rose felt like a warrior that day. Rose reached over her shoulder, patted herself on the back, and collapsed into sleep.

## CHAPTER 13
## *Ni Esrever*

*R*ose woke up the next morning feeling hot and itchy and confused.

More bizarre and frightening things had happened to her yesterday than happen to a typical person during her whole lifetime. She was looking forward to going downstairs and having just a plain old regular day.

Her only tasks until her parents returned were to see that the bakery ran smoothly and to make sure no one tinkered with the book. That way, when they came back, they would see that the kitchen was clean, Leigh's hair was washed, Ty and Sage had all of their limbs, and Rose was worthy of being entrusted with the family secrets.

Rose threw on her favorite T-shirt, one with pink and orange stripes, and splashed some water on her face. Her skin was peppered with inflamed red pimples. This happened a lot in the summer, when Rose was harried from working at the bakery and sweating constantly in the process.

There was a knock on the bathroom door. "Just a minute!" Rose called out. She leaned forward into the mirror, studying her zits. She needed some of Lily's magic potion.

As though summoned, the voice called out, "It's your aunt Lily! May I come in?"

Before Rose could say no, that she was fine by herself, Aunt Lily opened the door and sauntered inside.

"Good morning," Aunt Lily said. She plopped

a black toiletry bag on the counter. "Time to get to work!"

"I know," Rose said, studying her aunt's outfit—a short-sleeved purple top and a pair of slim-fitting jeans. Aunt Lily looked casual yet elegant. Rose glanced down at her own shirt and wasn't sure that stripes were such a good choice, after all. "Time to start baking."

"That's not the kind of work I meant." Aunt Lily unzipped her bag, and Rose could see that it was full of makeup. Purdy never let Rose wear any sort of makeup, claiming that it made girls look "as unappetizing as one of those Stetson donuts." But Rose had always secretly wondered if maybe a tiny bit of makeup—a little glamour—was exactly what she was missing.

"Staying pretty isn't easy, of course," Aunt Lily said. "I never used to wear makeup at all. I liked the *au naturel* look. But then someone told me that my lips looked like a turkey's, and from that day on I've never gone without some lipstick." Rose watched, transfixed, as Aunt Lily outlined her lips with a red pencil. "Even Chapstick works in a pinch. Anything shiny will do."

As Aunt Lily applied the rest of her makeup, her already beautiful face began to look even more beautiful. And Rose couldn't help but think of that voice in the pantry, the voice that told her that she would never be beautiful or powerful or important—the voice that somehow knew her deepest fear: that she would never be enough.

Aunt Lily was still a suspicious character, but she was also the first person in Rose's life who understood what it was to be a vibrant, smart, and beautiful woman. Maybe Aunt Lily could teach her what she needed to know so that Rose could grow up and be a vibrant, smart, and beautiful woman too.

"Aunt Lily?" Rose found herself asking.

"Yes, dear?"

"Do you think, maybe . . . you could do my . . . I mean, help me with . . . um?"

Aunt Lily stopped applying mascara midstroke

and said, "You'd like me to help you look beautiful?"

Rose nodded.

"Darling," Aunt Lily said, her voice a gentle purr, "I thought you'd never ask."


Rose waltzed into the kitchen feeling like a million dollars. Well, she actually had no idea what a million dollars felt like—but she felt good.

Pretty.

Chip was already there, dusting a replacement seven-layer cake with handfuls of fluffy coconut.

"Good morning!" Rose said.

"You know, Rose—I cleaned for five hours yesterday," Chip grumbled. "I had to pick a librarian's dentures off the floor. That is not part of my job description."

"I'm so sorry about that, Chip. I don't know what got into those gals. The older ones *or* the younger ones."

Just then, Chip looked up from the cake. "You

look . . . different, Rosie."

Rose glanced at Aunt Lily, who had a smile stretched across her face. "I think she looks just like herself," Aunt Lily said. "Only a bit . . . brighter."

Rose liked the sound of that. A bit brighter. "I'll go open the bakery. There's probably already a line out there." Rose glided through the saloon doors, wearing a friendly smile in anticipation of the multitude of friendly customers waiting to greet her.

But there was no multitude.

There wasn't even a modest multitude.

There wasn't a single customer. No Mr. Bastable, no Miss Thistle, or Mrs. Havegood; no teachers, no librarians, no summer-school students.

No one.

"What do we need, Rose? More muffins?" said Aunt Lily, gliding into the front room. "Oh dear. Seems no one's here yet."

Chip hurled his tanned, muscled torso into the front room to see for himself, a pile of shredded coconut in each hand. "Huh," he said. "That's weird. Thursday is usually our busiest morning."

"Yes! Bizarre!" Aunt Lily said. "Almost as if something were amiss."

Rose shrugged nervously. "Just wait," she said. "They'll come. Oh, they're definitely coming." Rose quietly consolidated a few nearly empty trays of muffins, adjusted the seven-layer cakes in their handsome glass stands, and then swept the black-and-white tile floor under the swirling wrought-iron café chairs, even though Chip had thoroughly swept the day before. She even shook out the old brown welcome mat.

And then Rose planted herself behind the counter and waited.

Three hours went by, and still no one had passed through the bakery, except for Mrs. Carlson, who had come downstairs to announce that Leigh was "a lazy mollusk" who refused to wake up, and that Mrs. Carlson herself would have to miss a day of tanning so that she could stay inside and watch the child until she had the decency to get out of bed. Then she had taken one look at Rose and her new look, harrumphed, and gone back upstairs.

No one had passed in *front* of the bakery, not even in a car. Rose had called her friend Alexandra to hang out, like she promised herself she'd do, but no one had answered. It was like the world had stopped moving and the Bliss house just hadn't gotten the memo.

Chip abandoned baking for the day and sat in the kitchen doing a Sudoku puzzle. Aunt Lily wiped down the glass front of the counter for a third time that morning while Rose did some math in her head:

Ty had gotten back from delivering the last of the cakes around ten. It was noon now. The recipe said the cake took twelve hours to reach its maximum potential. So why had no one come to the bakery? Were they too satiated from eating cake the night before to even think about buying muffins? Who was ever too full for a muffin?

Just then, Ty and Sage came downstairs, both dressed in matching blue button-down dress shirts, their hair gelled into matching red faux hawks. Sage looked like a shrunken version of Ty, with rounder cheeks.

"Don't you both look handsome!" said Aunt Lily.

The moment they saw Rose, they spoke at the same time. "What's wrong?"

"Jinx!" cried Sage.

"No one says that anymore," Rose said.

"You look different." Ty walked a circle around Rose, crossing his arms in front of his chest. "What is it?"

Rose couldn't help but smile. "Why don't you guess?"

"I know!" said Sage. "You're not wearing any underwear!"

Rose shook her head. "Wrong. Try again."

"New shirt?" Ty grimaced. "No, you've had that ugly striped thing forever."

"*No!*" Could her brothers really not tell what was different? "I'm wearing makeup!"

"Oh, is that all?" said Ty, instantly bored. "Is that why the bakery isn't open? Because you put on makeup?"

"No. What does makeup have to do with the bakery?"

"I don't know," he said, picking up a muffin and sniffing it. "It's just strange that no one's here."

"Exactly—*no one* came to the bakery this morning," Rose began, trying not to get too upset in front of Aunt Lily. "Not one single person. Which is weird. I think maybe something is, you know"—she winked— "*wrong.*" Her lip trembled a little. It was scary to admit that something might be wrong after having been so thoroughly and comfortably convinced that all was, at last, right.

"Maybe they blocked off the street 'cause they're filming an episode of *Law & Order* or something!" Sage volunteered, pumping a fist into the air.

Ty went to the window and peeked around the corner, where the only movement came from a lazy July breeze rustling through their neighbor's hedges. He turned to her and scratched the back of his neck, which was something Ty did only when he was genuinely concerned. "You're right: It's weird. Let's just pop into the town square to make sure everything is copacetic, okay? Just to soothe our minds?"

"Aunt Lily," Rose asked, in the sort of calm, professional voice that her guidance counselor used to help her plan out her class schedule, "would you mind manning the counter while we pop over to the town square for a minute?"

Aunt Lily used the same voice. "I don't mind at all! Go forth and prosper!"

Standing in the center of the town square, Rose's mind was anything but soothed.

On the way, they'd passed by a quiet school, an empty church parking lot, a deserted firehouse, and a people's court with no people. Cars sat abandoned in driveways. Rows of storefronts were a blur of red and white signs bearing the same seven ugly letters: CLOSED.

The brick plaza of the town square was hot and empty as a desert. Rose could see the heat rising off the statue of Reginald Calamity and the roof of Pierre Guillaume's and the silver awning of Calamity Cream, but no one was tossing coins in the fountain, waiting for *coq au vin*, or selling scoops of coffee ice cream.

Rose spun around when she heard a scuffle from across the plaza, hoping that it was a person.

But no. It was just a pigeon, a fat gray pigeon waddling over the brick searching desperately for crumbs from sandwiches and potato chips that weren't being eaten on this hot, still, alien day.

"I don't get it," said Sage. "Shouldn't everyone be back to normal?"

Ty nervously scratched the back of his neck with one hand and his smooth chin with the other. "Maybe everyone just overslept! Heck—me and Sage did! Maybe they'll be up by dinnertime."

But by seven o'clock that evening, still no one had stirred—including Leigh, who had been snoring contentedly for over twenty-four hours. Mrs. Carlson had called the doctor at four to ask what might be the matter, but no one had answered. At around five p.m., Chip went home for the day, declaring, "Well, *that* was a waste! I could have done my laundry today."

As the sky began to darken, Aunt Lily cornered Rose in the kitchen.

"Something is wrong. It seems that everyone in town has either taken a sleeping pill or has fallen under the spell of a wicked witch."

Rose was heartened by the thought that perhaps there *was* an actual wicked witch in Calamity Falls who had caused some sleeping enchantment, but her heart sank again when she realized that the wicked witch was, in fact, Rose Bliss.

"This wouldn't have anything to do with the cake

that you all distributed to the entire town yesterday, would it? The one that 'fixed everything?'" Aunt Lily's voice was an unsettling mix of worry and anger.

Rose drooped as she thought of how thoroughly she had broken her parents' rules. Her only goal for the week had been to prove to her parents that she was worthy of their respect, of using the family cookbook, of being a real baker.

Instead, she had cooked up a huge mess, a mess so dark and deep that being at the center of it felt a lot like being at the bottom of a swamp.

As if Lily could read her mind, she said, "Rose, I know what it's like to feel like everyone else outshines you, like you need to scream for their attention. I used to be an entirely plain person—then I discovered baking. You and I both bake because we enjoy it, but we also bake because we want to be extraordinary. And sometimes when you're trying to be extraordinary, you go too far. Do you know what I mean?"

Rose nodded. No one had ever put it so succinctly.

And for putting it so succinctly, Rose felt that perhaps Lily wouldn't judge her if she just buckled down
and told the truth. She began with a big breath.

"Well, it started when we made some Love Muffins
and gave them to Mr. Bastable and Miss Thistle and
then we made Cookies of Truth and tried to give them
to Mrs. Havegood but Chip accidentally gave them
out to everyone in the town including the librarians,
who had a catfight in the lobby of the bakery, and
then Ty gave Love Muffins and Cookies of Truth to
all the girls in his class because I think beneath it all
he's kind of insecure and attention-seeking like everyone else, and the girls went crazy like they were at a
Justin Bieber concert and they all fainted but we gave
them a Turn-Around-Inside-Out-Upside-Down Cake
that reversed everything we did before and then Ty
gave the Upside-Down Cake to every single person in
town so they'd go back to normal and basically we had
it covered, but now I'm thinking maybe something
might have gone a little bit wrong because the town

seems to have, you know, frozen. . . ." Rose drifted off as she huffed for air. She'd expected to feel a wonderful lightness after sharing the truth, but instead she felt shooting stomach pains.

Lily held Rose's cheeks in her soft hands. "Rose, you are incredible. You are quite simply the cleverest, most talented young person I have ever seen. There is true greatness in you."

Rose wanted to freeze that moment and live in it, like a dollhouse. She couldn't remember ever feeling so filled with potential. She felt like gold was coursing through her veins. She didn't question why Lily was being so encouraging, so complimentary. She just wanted to bottle the feeling and take a sip each morning before floating out of bed and skipping gracefully through the day.

"But," Aunt Lily went on, snapping Rose out of her euphoria, "part of greatness is admitting when you need help. And if something has gone wrong, there's a chance I can help. I do have some *experience* with this sort of thing." Lily's eyes went wide, and Rose couldn't help but wonder if Lily meant that she had experience with baking, or with managing magical disasters.

There was no time to wonder, because at that moment they heard Mrs. Carlson screaming from upstairs. "Help! It's Leigh!"

Rose and Lily ran upstairs and found Mrs. Carlson hunched over on the hall carpet, pinning Leigh to the floor. Leigh didn't seem to mind—she just giggled happily and flailed her arms. Sage arrived in the hall a moment later, panting.

"Where's Ty?" asked Rose.

"Taking out the garbage," Sage answered. "Geez, Louise! What's wrong with Leigh?"

"The child is possessed! Call the priest!" Mrs. Carlson shouted in her thick brogue.

"She looks fine!" Rose cried.

"I'm telling you, Satan has invaded her soul!"

"Oh, nonsense," Lily said, gently pulling Mrs. Carlson away.

"Release me, harlot! The child must be contained!"

And then Rose understood what Mrs. Carlson was ranting about: Once she was free, Leigh got up on all fours and began to shuffle backward over the carpet of the upstairs hallway, butt first, like a lamb being herded backward into a pen.

Then Leigh opened her mouth, and the weird got even weirder. "Ym eman si Yelsrap!" she gurgled. "Ym eman si Yelsrap!"

Sage pointed to Leigh and said, "Whoa. I think she really *is* possessed!"

Suddenly from outside there came the sound of someone screaming. Rose and Sage and Lily rushed to the bathroom window, which overlooked the side of the house.

The scream had come from Ty, who was standing by the garbage cans, paralyzed with fear.

He was surrounded by a circle of eight men in gray uniforms, each hugging a bulging black plastic sack in his arms. Rose thought at first that the men were walking away from Ty, but it soon became clear that they were moving toward Ty—backward. These grown men were walking backward. All eight of them.

They planted their toes in the ground behind them and then rocked back onto their heels. Their heads faced forward. As the circle of men drew tighter around Ty, he huddled behind the trash cans and screamed for help.

But the men ignored him.

They simply dropped their sacks on the ground, then turned around and walked backward toward the street, one or another of them stumbling to the ground or bumping into a shrub every few feet. Through the window, Rose could finally see the labels on the breast pockets of their uniforms: CALAMITY FALLS SANITATION.

When finally they bumped into the side of their truck, all eight of them awkwardly piled backward into the cab, then drove—backward—to the next house, the truck beeping down the street.

"*That's* not right," Aunt Lily said. "Come on."

Downstairs, they flew out the backdoor and circled Ty.

"What was that all about?" Rose asked, brushing away a stray piece of garbage that had fallen on Ty's sleeve during the drop-off.

"Those garbage men just delivered garbage," said Ty, kicking at one of the bags. "They delivered it instead of doing what they're supposed to do: take it away."

"Is this even our garbage?" Sage asked. "It smells kind of funky."

"Why were they walking backward?" Rose asked.

Ty gasped, his lips forming an O. "I don't think that's all. Look!"

Rose gazed down the driveway at the street that, in the dark, had finally come to life. Lights had flickered on in all of the houses, and a few people in bathrobes were backing down their front walks, depositing their folded newspapers in the grass, and then walking backward inside again. A few garage doors were raised, and cars reversed out into the street, then swerved backward to the end of the block and around the corner. Mr. Roller was busily wiping dirt onto his Corvette with a muddy sponge, as Peter Strickland, the paperboy, slowly rolled his bike backward down the sidewalk, stopping every now and again to steal a newspaper off a lawn. Mrs. Burns dragged her sheltie down the opposite side of the street, a blue plastic bag in her hand.

"I don't even want to know what she's going to do with that dog," Ty said.

Across the street, Rose saw Mrs. Calhoun kiss little Kenny on the head and hand him his lunch box. Kenny ran off backward with his backpack in the direction of the elementary school.

"What is everyone doing?" she asked. "It's night-time! They should be getting ready for bed."

Lily smoothed Rose's bangs over her forehead. "It seems that the Turn-Around-Inside-Out-Upside-Down

Cake is doing just what it claimed to do."

"Yeah, I'm starting to think the Upside-Down cake was maybe not the best idea," Ty said, frowning. "In retrospect."

"So it's the cake's fault?" Sage asked.

"It's our fault," Rose said, feeling like she was going to throw up. She and Ty hadn't fixed everything— they'd made it worse.

Their next-door-neighbor Mrs. Daublin walked backward in front of the house wearing her muu-muu and turban. She looked at Rose with a friendly expression—a stark reversal for their very cranky neighbor. "Olleh, Esor!" she shouted, lifting one foot in the air and shaking it back and forth like she was waving. She lost her balance and fell to the pavement, laughing hysterically.

Rose paced to the end of the driveway and saw Mrs. Havegood speeding backward down the street in her silver Cadillac, then screech to a halt at a green light at the end of the block. She spotted Rose out her window and awkwardly managed to lift a foot out the window of the car and wiggle it, as Mrs. Daublin had. "ESOR!" she yelled. "M'I A LACIGOLOHTAP RIAL!" Then the light turned red, and she slammed on the gas and squealed down the road until she was out of sight.

*"Esor?"* said Rose. "What does that mean?"

Sage pulled a piece of chalk out of his pocket and wrote ESOR on the driveway. "Esor. Esor." Then he raised one finger in the air and gasped. "ESOR is ROSE backward! Everyone is talking backward!"

"So everyone is driving backward, talking backward, waving hello with their feet, and doing the opposite of what they usually do," said Rose, pulling at her hair.

Aunt Lily's eyes darted around nervously. "My goodness. You certainly have a situation on your hands."

"We should have made the recipe that sewed people's mouths shut instead," said Ty.

Rose watched in horror as her neighbors stumbled blindly through their morning routines, and she winced to see each one step backward, falter, and fall.

The four of them grew quieter and quieter on their walk into town. In the schoolyard, pigtailed and cowlicked summer-school students wagged stern fingers at their teachers, who were playing tag and building sand castles in their jackets and ties under the bright moon. At the firehouse, Fire Chief Conklin and his team were trying to climb up their fire pole, without much success. Construction workers unscrewed pieces of drywall from the frame of a house, a landscaper covered well-manicured lawns with heaps of cut grass, a toddler pulled his mother in a stroller. Retirees practicing tai chi in the park looked the same as always, until they tried to meditate on their heads.

In the town square, Rose walked with her aunt and her brothers past the Reginald Calamity fountain, where passersby were stepping into the water and fishing coins *out* of it. The librarians Mrs. Hackett and Mrs. Crisp were scooting around the plaza, stealing books from the hands of readers on the benches and carting them back to the library. At Pierre Guillaume's, Monsieur Guillaume himself waited hungrily, fork and knife in hand, while diners ferried plates of food from the kitchen to his table, backward, most of them tripping over themselves and sending gratins and fillets of sole and crèmes brûlées careening through the air.

"Am I mistaken," Aunt Lily said, "or did the woman just sell a plate of filet mignon *to* Monsieur Guillaume?"

Rose nodded slowly. "Yes."

"I can't watch this any longer," Aunt Lily said. "Something has to be done. I have an idea. Perhaps if we give everyone some warm milk it will encourage them to sleep. Sage, come conference with me a moment and tell me where I can get a hold of a lot of milk."

As Sage stepped to the side with Aunt Lily, Rose

stepped in close to Ty. "We have to call Mom and Dad. They're the only ones who will know what to do."

"No way," Ty said. "We'll get in so much trouble."

"I think we'll probably be in more trouble if we say nothing and Mom and Dad come home and get a ticket for driving *forward*," said Rose.

"Can't we just ask Aunt Lily for help?" Ty said. "She's one of us. She's even got that ladle on her shoulder. . . ."

Rose watched as Lily marched toward their house, tall and proud as a swan, the Bliss family birthmark pulsing as she moved her shoulders back and forth. Of all the people currently blubbering backward through Calamity Falls, Aunt Lily was certainly the one most likely to save the day. And Lily *was* one of them. Better still, she believed in Rose and had taken an interest in her talents and potential like no one ever had, not even her own mother. Still, there was some niggling fear that kept Rose from wanting the Cookery Booke to fall into Lily's hands. "I just—"

That's when Sage rejoined them, and Rose noticed that there was no longer any key glinting in the moonlight around Sage's neck.

"Sage!" Rose hissed, spitting his name out like it was something you couldn't say on TV. "Where is the key?"

Sage cowered and shielded his face with his puffy pink hands. "Don't hit me!" he screamed, even though he had never been hit in his life, except once by the rim of the trampoline on a jump gone wrong. "I gave it to Aunt Lily!"

"Why?" Rose screamed.

"Because she asked for it! Because we need her help! Because she knows what she's doing! She said she wanted to find a way to solve the problem with magic," Sage said, looking frightened. "I bet she's consulting the cookbook even as we speak."

Rose looked around and realized it was true: Aunt Lily was nowhere in sight.

## CHAPTER 14

# A New Cook in the Kitchen

ose, Ty, and Sage burst into the kitchen to find Lily leaning over the Bliss Cookery Booke, which lay splayed out on the countertop. She was wearing a button-up white dress with short sleeves and a collar that made her look like a lab technician or a World War II nurse, or both.

Rose's first instinct was to grab the book away, but Lily was leaning on it with her elbows so that there was no way of snatching it up. Besides, Rose saw something else that took the fight out of her: Aunt Lily had the whisk key dangling from her neck.

Then she spied the little red light on the answering machine blinking. "Did someone call?"

"Yes," Aunt Lily answered, not looking up from the book. "Your father. I encouraged Mrs. Carlson to let the machine get it. I didn't want to have to tell him what was going on. He said they're coming home the day after tomorrow, so if you burned the house down, you should fix it before then. His words, not mine."

Rose rubbed her forehead vigorously with her hands the way her mother did whenever she was truly upset. "I'm dead. That's it. I did everything wrong, and now I'm dead meat."

"Roooooose," Aunt Lily said, slowly folding her mouth around the word, like she was saying it for the benefit of someone who could only read lips. "We are a family. And we are going to fix this as a family.

Remember that part of greatness is admitting that you need help."

Rose slumped like an old rag doll, utterly defeated. She had failed: to help her town, to keep her little sister safe, to protect her family's most important possession. The Bliss Cookery Booke was even more important than their house. It was like a fifth child. And there it sat, out in the open, being squashed by someone Rose didn't entirely trust.

Still, she had to admit that seeing Lily there, strong and capable, standing over the book, came as something of a relief. At least now Rose wasn't the only one in charge.

"Now. Show me the recipe that made everyone crazy," said Lily. Ty and Sage rubbed their hands together like determined con artists and surrounded the chopping block. Ty flipped to the back cover, where the section labeled ALBATROSS'S APOCRYPHA lay nestled in its compartment.

As Lily lifted the booklet onto the table, Rose

noticed that the pages were fuzzy. Aunt Lily ran her fingers over the pages and found that they were covered in a gray dust that was neither ash, nor mold, but something else, something rotten. Lily looked genuinely shaken as she discreetly wiped her fingers on the side of her white nurse's dress.

"I'd heard about this section of the book," Lily muttered to herself, "but I thought it was just a legend."

Rose perked up and looked at Lily suspiciously. "I thought you said you never heard of the book."

Lily froze and backpedaled. "I . . . heard of my great-great-great-grandfather Albatross writing down some recipes of his own. And these must be them."

"Albatross's recipes are rank," said Sage, waving a hand in front of his nose.

Lily laughed. "Your great-great-great-uncle had a flair for darkness and mayhem," she said. "I'll bet all his recipes are like that. If we want to fix this town, we should probably look elsewhere in the book."

Lily closed the moldy gray booklet and nestled it

back into its hiding place, then took a deep breath and flipped to the very beginning of the book, turning the thick, creamy white pages one by one and studying the etchings in the margins. Winter-Warmth Cookies. Obedient-Children Mousse. Kickstart-a-Small-Business Carrot Cake. The more she read, the more the lines of her face filled with wonder. It seemed to Rose that Aunt Lily was growing younger and younger with each flip of the page. Her milky skin seemed to glow a little pinker and her eyes seemed to shimmer like ripples on a lake at sunset. The corners of her mouth were tacked into a plastic smile that seemed to Rose to smack more of greed than of joy.

"You know, it's amazing what this book could do," Aunt Lily murmured. "Did your parents ever think of sharing these recipes with the world? It's sort of unfair to keep them cooped up in that little room where only the Bliss family bakery can profit from them, don't you think?"

"Actually, they keep it locked in there to protect it from people who want to abuse its power," Rose said, knowing that Lily's mind was too lost in an ocean of possibilities to really hear her.

Lily turned to a page where there were two drawings in the margin, one of a town overrun by calamity—like Calamity Falls in its present state—and one of a town where everything looked happy and peaceful.

### Back-to-Before Blackberry Torte: For the Restitution of Prior Conditions

*It was in 1717 in Scotland that Sir Albatross Bliss did feed to the entire town of Tyree a slice of the Upside-Down Cake, and everyone did walk and speak in a manner most unbecoming. This was in order to ruin his brother Filbert's wedding ceremony. Filbert Bliss did leave the church and run to his kitchen, where he concocted this Blackberry Torte, which undid the chaos that Albatross wrought, and each attended the blessed wedding without remembering his prior folly.*

Aunt Lily looked down, embarrassed at her great-great-great-grandfather's bad behavior. "Looks like this ought to do the trick, hmm?" She read out the ingredients list:

*Filbert did mix four fists* **chocolate** *with one fist* **butter** *with one fist* **sugar** *and four of the* **chicken's eggs** *over a trouble boiler. Then he did coax the Dwarf of Perpetual Sleep from his perpetual sleep and bade him whisper the* **secret of time** *into the batter. He did bake for a TIME of* **eleven songs** *at a HEAT of* **five flames**. *He did top the torte with a sauce made from* **blackberries** *and* **sugar**.

Ty slapped Lily lightly on the shoulder. "Don't worry, *Tía* Lily." He laughed. "We're hip to the lingo vis-à-vis the fists and flames and songs and stuff."

"What on God's sweet earth is a *trouble boiler*?" Sage demanded, cocking his head to the side and tossing his arms stiffly in the air.

Aunt Lily stood straight, pointing out her toes as if she were a ballerina. "*That*," she announced, "is where having a magical baker for an aunt comes in handy! I know exactly what a trouble boiler is, and also how to use one. Fear not, young ones—we will be serving up this Back-to-Before Blackberry Torte in no time!"

Lily extended one of her hands into the air and then lowered it. Quickly, Ty and Sage gathered round and put their hands on top of Aunt Lily's like they were football teammates about surge onto the field.

"Rose?" Aunt Lily said, raising an eyebrow and motioning to their hands in the circle.

But something in Rose still wasn't sure that she wanted to place her hand on top of Aunt Lily's. She knew that she needed help, and Aunt Lily certainly did seem capable. But she had seen the glow on Aunt

Lily's face when she looked at the Cookery Booke— it was the kind of glow that meant Aunt Lily would do anything to have the recipes for herself. And Rose knew this because she had felt the same desire before.

Ty and Sage, though, were oblivious.

"Come on, Rose," Ty said, wrapping his free arm around her shoulders and pulling her in close. "We need you."

Rose looked at Sage, who was waiting for her to place her hand on top of his as well. She didn't want to let them down—not now, when they needed her the most. She'd already failed her parents. There was no way she was going to fail her family.

"We can't do it without you, Rose. We need your talents," Aunt Lily said.

This was the final nail. For the first time in her life, Rose felt pretty. And important. And powerful. She didn't want those feelings to end—not yet.

And so, despite her hesitations, Rose placed her stubby fingers on top of Aunt Lily's long and elegant ones.

As soon as she did, they all pumped their hands up and down. Aunt Lily said, "All for one—let's get this done!"

And they were off.

Lily sent Sage and Ty off to Poplar's for one hundred dozen eggs, fifty pounds of chocolate, and every blackberry in town. "We need enough for everyone!"

"How will we pay for it?" Ty asked.

Aunt Lily pondered a minute. "Tell them that you are rival grocers. They'll do the opposite of what they're supposed to, which is give their food away for free! Do you have anything that looks like what a grocery clerk would wear?"

Before Lily could finish, Ty was shouting, "I worked at a grocery store for three days once and I still have the uniform!" And he ran up to his room and came down wearing a green apron with a visor on it that said PIGGLY WIGGLY.

Lily giggled and said, "Go forth and conquer, men!"

Ty looked at the tiny red wagon. "It's going to take a lot of trips," he muttered. Then he and Sage rolled down the driveway to the road, leaving Rose and Lily alone in the kitchen.

Rose had to admit it: There was something sweetly outrageous about Aunt Lily, how beautiful and in control she was, with just a slight hint of danger. Today Rose felt closer to her aunt than she ever had before. Maybe she needed a role model like Aunt Lily around all the time, someone to help her become fabulous and respected.

They could hear Mrs. Carlson desperately trying to calm Leigh in her room. "Devil spawn! Stop your yapping! Why won't you sleep!"

Rose and Aunt Lily looked at each other nervously.

"There's not much time," Lily said. "We need to build a trouble boiler, stat. I have never built one, but I saw one used once, at a family reunion. It was a giant cauldron set inside an even larger cauldron filled with boiling water."

"How giant?"

"Giant."

Rose wandered into the backyard and looked around at the refuse that lay near the shed. An old metal rowboat. The freshly torn trampoline. A huge metal satellite dish that had gotten fried in an electrical storm, which Albert had never had the heart to throw away.

After a minute, it all clicked. "I know!" said Rose.

What followed was this: Rose and Aunt Lily set to work rigging the biggest trouble boiler that had ever been rigged. They pulled the broken skin from the trampoline and made a fire underneath the frame, using some logs and old newspaper. They washed out the old metal rowboat and set it on top, and they filled it with water. And then they washed out the huge broken satellite dish that Albert had ordered and set that afloat on the water in the rowboat.

Aunt Lily patted Rose on the back. "As they say in England, Rose—brilliant."

All the dark suspicions that Rose harbored about Aunt Lily this past week dissolved in the light of her praise.

Eventually, the boys pulled into the driveway with their last wagonload filled with eggs and chocolate and blackberries. Sage got to work dumping the pounds of chocolate into the satellite dish and cracking hundreds of eggs. Aunt Lily controlled the head on the fire, and Ty and Sage alternated stirring with one of the old oars from the rowboat. Rose mostly just watched as little sparks from the fire crackled up into the dark of the warm night sky. Trouble boilers were one thing, but she and her brothers baking together, laughing together, on a Thursday night in July? Now *that* was magic.

After all the ingredients had been combined and Rose had stuffed the enormous mound of eggshells into a garbage bag, it was time to pull out the big guns.

"Let's go get that dwarf," Rose said.

Rose turned the rolling-pin handle. The floorboards detached, and a musty stench rose up into the chill of the refrigerator.

"The dwarf is down there," Rose said, leading Aunt Lily by the hand. When they were down in the chamber, Lily waved her flashlight past jars of earth, wind, and fire, flapping butterfly wings, and talking mushrooms.

Rose felt the wet mist from the grate lap at her ankles.

Lily must have felt it too, because she stepped in the direction of the grate and knelt in front of it. Rose couldn't hear it saying anything, but then again, when the thing beneath the house spoke to her, it hadn't really made a sound.

Aunt Lily scrambled away a moment later and looked gravely at Rose.

"Are you all right?" Rose asked.

"Sure. It's just a little cold in here." Lily turned her attention to the collection of jars on the walls, each of which glowed a little brighter as she passed. She approached a jar with a giant dragonfly inside labeled FLIGHT. The dragonfly cowered at the back of its jar as she passed. "This is quite the impressive collection.

Not all magic is wands and spells and potions, you know. Some of it—the best kind, I think—is much subtler. Like this."

Rose was elated by what Aunt Lily said. She'd put into words exactly what Rose felt. Her parents never talked about magic at all; they just did it. But maybe Aunt Lily was right: Maybe it *was* selfish of Rose's parents to keep the Cookery Booke locked away in a tiny bakery in a tiny town. What good could it do here? Maybe there was magic that needed to be done beyond Calamity Falls—subtle magic, gentle magic—that could make the world a better place.

And maybe Rose could be the one to work that magic.

Aunt Lily let the flashlight settle on the jar where the Dwarf of Perpetual Sleep sat inside, snoring. "*Look* at him! He's *gorgeous*!"

Rose wouldn't go so far as to call him gorgeous, but he certainly was interesting to look at. He wore a pointed green cap on his head, and fuzzy white hair exploded from beneath it like the head of a dandelion. Lily handed Rose the flashlight and gingerly took the jar from the shelf, cradling it in the crook of her arm like a newborn, then she tiptoed up the stairs, whispering all the time to the jar, "Don't worry, little one! No harm will come to you! My little dwarf! My wonderful little fellow!"

Lily set the jar on the chopping block and stared into it. "Have you ever seen anything so marvelous?"

Rose stared through the tinted blue glass of the mason jar at the withered old face of the dwarf. He was wearing a little coat made of brown felt and tan long johns. He was about the size of a Cabbage Patch Kids doll. His eyes were squeezed shut, yielding an explosion of crow's-feet at the corners.

Rose held the jar while Lily slid her hands under the dwarf's armpits and gently lifted him out. The air inside the jar was stale, and it seeped from the jar and filled the kitchen. Lily sat him on the chopping block. He continued to snore, and, in his slumber, slowly leaned too far to the right and—*thwap!*—bonked his head on the chopping block.

That woke the dwarf right up.

He shook his head out and righted himself crankily, then raised his little arms in the air and yawned, revealing a spotted tongue and toothless old gums.

His breath was nearly impossible to describe. It was rank. It smelled like garbage and old fish and poop.

The Bliss children all gagged and backed away as far as they could as the putrid wind from the yawning dwarf filled the room. Rose pinched her nose as hard as she could until the smell died down.

When Rose managed to open her eyes again, she found the dwarf staring at her, arms crossed in front of his chest, one foot tapping. "I suppose you've woken me from my slumber because you need me to whisper a *secret* into some *batter*."

"Yes . . . ," Rose admitted. He was a quick one, this dwarf.

"Which one?" he snarled.

Aunt Lily said, "The secret of time?"

The dwarf scratched his chin for a minute, thinking deeply. "The secret of time . . . the secret of time . . ." Then he snapped his head up and announced tragically, "I have forgotten the secret of time!"

Rose's heart sank. After all the work they'd done, to have their dreams of Blackberry Tortes dashed because of an old dwarf's faulty memory.

Then the dwarf snickered. "Ha! I had you! I'm kidding. Of *course* I know the secret of time. Puh-lease."

"Oh, thank you, Dwarf of Perpetual Sleep!" cried Rose. Under normal circumstances she would have hugged him, but he smelled too foul to be approached.

"I have a name," he said crossly. "Rude."

"I'm so sorry, I didn't mean to be."

"No, my *name* is Rude. Rude Dingherwurst."

Rude spotted Aunt Lily staring lovingly at him from the corner. "I will whisper the secret of time if *she*," he pointed at Lily, "will hold me over the batter."

Aunt Lily bowed. *"Anything* for you, Mr. Dingherwurst."

"If you drop me, you will have to marry me," he said, snickering. "No, seriously."

Lily laughed. "I just may drop you, then!" And she picked up the dwarf under his arms and strolled outside.

Rose and her brothers gathered around the steaming satellite dish, while Aunt Lily held Mr. Rude Dingherwurst over the molten chocolate.

"Ow!" he winced. "Steam in the face! A little farther away, darlin'!"

Aunt Lily moved him back a few inches.

"Ready?" Aunt Lily said. Rose could tell that she was trying to be as sweet as possible.

"Almost." He coughed. "I'd love a foot rub first. And a shot of whiskey. Whatever you have is fine, although I'd prefer an audience with Mr. Johnny Walker."

That was enough. Rose was not about to let the rudeness of Mr. Rude Dingherwurst spoil their whole operation. She couldn't flirt like Aunt Lily, but she could give him a piece of her mind.

Rose went up to the molten chocolate bowl and put her nose just one inch from Mr. Rude Dingherwurst's. "Pardon me, Mr. D. We are in some serious trouble right now. We're sorry we've interrupted your nap, but that's no reason at all to waste our time. If you're not going to help us, that's fine. Because I'd rather live in a town where everything is upside down than have to rub what I'm sure are your very, very smelly feet." Rose had always wanted to make a dramatic speech like that but never had occasion to before. "If you don't mind."

Rude didn't say anything; he just grumbled and turned back to the batter. Then he whispered something in a language Rose didn't understand.

*Maireann croi eadrom I bhfad.*

Then he pulled his head back and said, "There. Now may I go back to sleep, please?"

His whisper hung in the air over the trouble boiler

in a stream of bloodred mist that spilled over the chocolate and became like the two hands of a clock, seeming to stir the batter like paddles as they whirred counterclockwise. They turned and turned around within the satellite dish, whooshing and gurgling and ticking, like a clock made of goopy chocolate was being wound backward.

Around them, the world shivered and rippled, the air warping like melting plastic. Rose realized her breath was caught in her chest, and try as she might, she couldn't open her mouth—the moment of time seemed to stretch out and stretch out until she thought she'd suffocate if she couldn't breathe—when with a *snap!* it was over, and she took in a long, raggedy wet breath.

She gasped, "What happened?"

Sage and Ty both coughed. "Beats me," Ty said.

And with that, Aunt Lily carried Mr. Rude Dingherwurst back to his jar and dunked him into the murky fluid (he winked as his head was submerged);

then Rose set him on the shelf downstairs, but not before hearing the sinister voice from beneath the grate.

*If you find the Tincture of Venus unappealing,* it said, *just clutch the apron strings of your aunt Lily. She knows the ways to fame and fortune and glamour beyond compare.*

Rose shivered and rushed back upstairs, sensing that the thing beneath the house somehow knew more than it was saying. Maybe Rose would return later and ask it what to do. But before she could do that, there were Blackberry Tortes to bake.

Aunt Lily ladled the batter into cake pans while Rose and Sage heated all the blackberries in the huge vat with more sugar. When the berries had boiled down into a delicious sugary mash, Rose spooned the mixture on top of the individual tortes as they came out of the oven.

"Now all we have to do is get everyone in town to

eat a slice of this," said Aunt Lily. "But how?"

"We'll just tell them they have to eat it, right?" Ty ventured.

Aunt Lily puzzled a moment. "No, that won't work. Whatever excuse we use to get people to eat this, it has to be backward, or else no one will listen."

"We could tell them to put it in their butts . . . ," Sage ventured.

Aunt Lily bonked him on top of the head. "That's not polite, Sage."

Again Rose had the solution. She could see herself getting used to this. "I know!" she announced. "We need the family van. And some serious speakers."

## CHAPTER 15

# Recipe the Fourth: Back-to-Before Blackberry Torte

*A*s soon as Rose said "speakers," Sage bolted up to his room. A minute later, he came careening down with two computer speakers. They were about the size of fuzzy dice that you'd hang off the rearview mirror of a car.

"Bigger," said Rose, making a pointed look at Ty. "Come on!"

Ty groaned. "I'm not carrying that thing. It's heavy!

Like, really heavy." Ty rolled up one of the sleeves of his T-shirt and flexed his bicep. Then he kissed it. "I might do some serious damage to this baby."

"What's the point of having muscles if you can't carry things with them?" Rose asked. "Besides, we finally found a use for your bass amp!"

Ty dragged himself upstairs. When he reappeared, he was sweating and panting and carrying the four-foot-tall amplifier that Purdy had bought him for his birthday. He had yet to use the amplifier because he had yet to open the electric bass that came along with it.

Rose nodded as she looked at the speaker, which was almost as tall as she was. "That's more like it."

"Care to elucidate the plan, Miss Rose?" asked Aunt Lily.

"What does *elucidate* mean?" Sage asked, scratching his forehead.

Aunt Lily threw up her arms. "It means to shed light on something! To explain!" At that, Lily ran around the room and threw on all of the overhead fluorescent lights, making the room as bright as a gym during a high-school basketball game. "Enlighten us, Rose!" she said. Rose couldn't help but giggle. Aunt Lily had a way of making even the bleakest of evenings feel like a party.

"Here's what we do," Rose said emphatically, swinging herself up onto the chopping-block table. "We tie the speaker up to the top of the van, and we plug a microphone in. Then we go around town and we tell everyone to stay *away* from the town square, that there is *not* a disco dance party there."

Aunt Lily clapped. "I see what you're doing here."

"I'll do the announcing," said Ty. "That way I can practice my radio voice."

Rose nodded at her brother. "Sure, Ty. As I was saying, that will naturally make everyone rush immediately to the town square for a disco dance party. And we'll be parked in the town square playing disco music under a sign begging people *not* to take our Blackberry Tortes. Which of course will compel everyone to take one."

Aunt Lily gave Rose a one-armed hug. "I adore any plan that involves a disco dance party. Smart thinking. Good job, Rosie!"

Delighted, Rose slid to the floor and took a bow. Even Ty and Sage had to hand it to her: It was a solid plan.

Aunt Lily winced as she drove the rusty old van through the dimly lit, twisted streets of Calamity Falls. "This is like a video game, only we could actually die."

Lily wasn't exaggerating. She was the only person driving forward.

Though she was an expert motorcyclist, Lily hadn't actually driven a car in years, she told the Bliss children, and she didn't feel comfortable winding through the narrow streets of an unfamiliar town in the middle of the night while driving in reverse. Rose gulped in the backseat along with Sage as Aunt Lily darted in between cars going the wrong way on the wrong side of the street, cars that had been parked willy-nilly into the street, and cars that had been backed into trees and fences and abandoned on the side of the road. Rose could see that even Ty was nervous—he clutched his seat belt with both hands in the front passenger seat.

As Principal Fanner drove past, he shook his fist out his window, slammed on the horn and screamed, "GNORW YAW!"

"What is he shouting at me?" Aunt Lily cried, stopping the van for a second to take a breath and smooth her short black hair.

Sage, the designated translator, wrote the curious phrase on the dry-erase board he'd taken down from the fridge. "Wrong way. He's yelling at you for going the wrong way!"

Lily stuck her full torso out of the driver's window and shouted defiantly, "No, buster, *you're* going the wrong way!"

Instead of shouting back, Mr. Fanner cowered nervously in the driver's seat as he slowly rolled past.

"Just pretend you're in London," Rose quipped.

Meanwhile, in the backseat, Sage had written out a message for the confused citizens of Calamity Falls: ON OCSID YTRAP NI NWOT ERAUQS! OD TON OG OT NWOT ERAUQS!, or, in plain English, *No disco party in town square! Do not go to town square!*

"How the heck do I say this?" Ty whined, clutching a microphone that he'd attached to the amp on the roof.

"Just sound it out!" Rose said, secretly glad that Ty had insisted on doing the announcing.

Ty rolled down his window, cleared his throat into the microphone, and began: "Umm . . . ummm. *On ock-sid ee-trap n-ee en-wot e-rowks.*" He glanced back at Rose with a bewildered, skeptical look. "This is harder than it looks!"

"Ty! You just broadcast that!"

He looked at the mic in his hand. "Whoops! *Eeerross!*" he said.

"Good!" Rose said, trying to be encouraging. She'd never seen Ty nervous about anything before. "Keep going!"

"There's no way this is right," he muttered, then began again. *"O-dd ton o-gg o-tt en-wot e-rowks."* The whole sentence came out a little smoother that time, even though the whole thing still sounded sort of like Ty trying not to throw up. English was not pretty in reverse.

"What do I do now?" he asked, closing his eyes and taking a deep breath, then opening them.

"Say it again!" said Rose. "Just say it over and over! With passion!"

"I love passion!" Aunt Lily said as she drove.

"This is so stupid," Ty grumbled. "It's not going to work."

"You're doing great," Rose whispered. She reached forward and patted his shoulder.

"Fine," Ty grumbled. *"On ok-sid ee-trap n-ee en-wot e-rowks."*

They drew up alongside Mrs. Havegood. She was driving backward in the left lane while Lily was driving forward in the right lane.

Right after Ty's announcement, Mrs. Havegood jammed on the brakes and peered over the solid yellow line into the Blissmobile. "YLLAER?!" which Rose immediately understood to mean *Really*?!

"Everyone shake your heads no," Rose said. They all dutifully waggled their heads back and forth.

Then Mrs. Havegood parked her car in the middle of the road and hurried backward on foot in the direction of the town square.

"It's working!" said Rose. "Looks like Mrs. Havegood loves herself some disco music!"

"Who doesn't?" said Aunt Lily, keeping her eyes on the road but dancing a little in her seat. "Disco party, here we come!"

Ty smiled, lifted the mic to his lips, and spoke again. And again. And again.

As they passed the school playground, Ty stuck his head out the window and proclaimed, "*On ok-sid *ee-trap n-ee en-wot e-rowks!"* The teachers abandoned their swinging and sliding and sandcastle building and backpedaled in the direction of the town square.

They pulled up in front of a construction site, and Ty actually got out of the van to announce, *"On ok-sid ee-trap n-ee en-wot e-rowks!"*

The workers cheered, tossed their hard hats into the air, and stopped their work filling holes and tearing things down, then stumbled backward through the streets.

Mailmen tossed their bags of letters into the night air and scooted backward over the terrain. Lawyers and accountants and pharmacists all looked up from the desks in their storefronts and flocked to the center of town, not bothering to lock their doors.

Apparently everyone in Calamity Falls really liked disco. Or maybe they *didn't* like disco. It hurt Rose's head to try to figure it out.

By the time they reached the base of Sparrow Hill, Ty was shouting out the backward English as smoothly as a DJ and as fast as a cattle auctioneer. *"On ok-sid ee-trap n-ee en-wot e-rowks!"* he said, in a gruff, sultry voice that would indeed be perfect for radio. He had completed the transformation by donning a pair of sunglasses and popping his collar.

Rose's pulse quickened as they mounted the hill past Kline's Key shop and parked in front of their last stop: Stetson's Donuts and Automotive Repair.

The hodgepodge old shop at the top of the hill was so dark and quiet that it looked like no one had lived there in years.

*"O-dd ton o-gg o-tt en-wot e-rowks!"* Ty called.

Rose waited a second, breathless, sucking in the cool night air like her life depended on it, waiting for Devin to emerge.

But no one in the repair shop came out.

Their van was gone, but Rose hadn't seen it parked haphazardly in any of the side streets. Come to think of it, she hadn't seen Devin all week, though she'd been too wrapped up in all the chaos to notice. They must have gone on vacation.

"Let's go," said Rose, both disappointed and relieved. "They're not here."

But Sage had already gotten out of the van and run to the overlook point at the top of Sparrow Hill, so Rose ran to fetch him back into the van.

There were no trees at the top of the hill, just the open sky, which tonight felt so vast and so black and so empty that Rose thought she might just get sucked up into it. It was breathtaking.

"Look!" Sage said, pointing to the clearing in the center of town where Reginald Calamity's marble doppelganger stood.

A few thousand people who looked no larger than beetles from this distance were milling around the brick plaza. The rumble of a collective whine rose from the square. They had all dropped what they were doing and rushed to a disco party with no disco music.

"It's time to give the people what they want!" Rose shouted. She was going to make things right. She was going to prove that she was worthy of the name *Bliss*.

Aunt Lily rolled into the town square blasting the soundtrack to *Saturday Night Fever*. They couldn't figure out a way to play the music backward, but apparently disco music sounds the same no matter which way you play it, because Mrs. Havegood, standing in a leopard-print dress that she was wearing inside out, screamed, "YAY! OCSID!"

People swaggered backward over the brick, awkwardly planting one foot and moving their pointed hands up and down in a diagonal on the wrong beat. Mr. Fanner collided butt first with Miss Karnopolis, and the two screamed at each other. Mr. Bastable and Miss Thistle spotted each other from across the crowd and plowed backward toward one another in time with the music, knocking over entire families. Children had formed a circle around Mrs. Havegood and cheered at her as she rolled around on the ground and did a mixed-up version of the worm. The moon served as an impromptu disco ball. The whole thing was beautiful in a sort of disturbing way.

Rose and Lily pushed all of Pierre Guillaume's outdoor dining tables into one massive banquet table, and Sage and Ty laid out all of the Back-to-Before Blackberry Tortes in a long line. They cut the tortes into slices and plopped each onto paper plates.

Rose was patiently awaiting her first noncustomer when, out of the corner of her eye, she spotted Devin Stetson floating listlessly in a darkened corner of the square, alone.

Aunt Lily caught her staring at the blond boy. "Who's that?" she asked.

Rose was too shy to answer.

"Why don't you go dance with him?"

Rose shook her head no. "We've never even had a real conversation."

"Well, this is a perfect opportunity to try it out, because he won't remember it in the morning!"

"I don't think he'd like me very much."

"Who wouldn't like you? You're beautiful, you're talented, you're going places."

Rose couldn't quite believe that Aunt Lily meant what she said, but still, the words sounded lovely, and they propelled Rose forward. If she was ever going to speak to Devin, tonight was the night. She felt somewhat invincible.

She made her way through the mob to where Devin Stetson was dancing. He wasn't attempting to plow through any real disco moves like the others; he was just sort of stepping back and forth. Rose stood facing him and mirrored his movements. He looked up in surprise.

"Ih," he said.

"Ih."

"Uoy kool ssorg," he said, which she flipped around in her head and took to mean "You look gross." On any other day this would have made her run to the nearest bathroom and whimper silently inside the stall, but on this special night she took it to mean that she looked pretty good.

Rose wished she had a mirror to check and see if the makeup Aunt Lily had helped her put on was still there, but she didn't. So she assumed that it was and smiled. "Sknaht," she said. "Uoy oot."

Then Devin turned around and sort of pushed the back of his head into her cheek, which, she supposed, was his backward attempt at a kiss. She melted at the touch of his baby-fine blond hair on her face. He smelled like soap and dreams.

From the corner of her eye, she could glimpse Aunt Lily standing behind the table at Pierre Guillaume's, giving her a thumbs-up.

Just as Rose had closed her eyes and fully embraced the beauty of this moment, backward though it was, Ty came up behind her and tapped her on the shoulder.

"Excuse me, *mi hermana*. I'm sorry to interrupt your fun, but no one is eating the cake."

Then Rose remembered a pivotal part of her plan that she'd forgotten about. If they wanted people to take free cake, they would need a sign.

She tore herself away from Devin's soft blond hair. Whatever happened after this—if he went back to ignoring her at school, if he didn't know her name— she'd remember this moment forever. "Eyb, Nived," she said, and then she was off.

Rose and Ty tilted over one Pierre Guillaume's huge white umbrellas, while Sage, the expert in backward print, dipped his finger in a bowl of leftover black-berry topping and smeared it over the white umbrella, writing:

## EW ERA YRGNUH! OD TON EKAT
## RUO EKAC!

Rose and Sage turned the umbrella it on its side on top of one of the tables. Ty ran to the van and made the announcement into the microphone, just to get every-thing started. *"O-dd ton ee-kat ru-oh e-kak!"* Then he cut the music.

If there was ever a need for a radio DJ to speak backward, Ty would be more than qualified for the job.

Mrs. Havegood was the first to see the umbrella sign near Pierre Guillaume's. She pointed at the sign and screamed, "KOOL! EKAC!"

Mrs. Havegood walked backward toward the table, then got on all fours and crawled backward under it, so that she was facing the cake, then she took a slice and devoured it. "EKAC!" she cried, beating her chest like a baboon.

And with that, she picked up individual slices of cake and sent them hurtling like footballs into the crowd. "OG GNOL!" she howled.

Meanwhile, the teachers and librarians seized their slices of cake and, after shoving them into their mouths, smeared the excess chocolate all over their faces, then grabbed all the empty cake pans and licked them clean as they hooted and stomped through the square.

Mr. Bastable and Miss Thistle caught two of the slices that Mrs. Havegood had sent airborne and fed them to each other. The rest of the crowd surrounded the tables like pigs at a slop trough. They didn't bother to pick up the cake—they bent their heads to their plates and ate without their hands.

Rose wondered when this terrifying display would give way to the normal human behavior that the torte recipe had promised.

She didn't have to wonder long.

Miss Karnopolis the librarian was the first to come to. She shook her head and saw her fellow librarians' heads buried in cake pans, then felt the sticky blackberry syrup she'd smeared on her face.

Then she noticed that it was the middle of the night.

"Oh my!" she exclaimed. "What am I doing awake! It's well past my bedtime! And why is my face covered in"—she wiped a finger over her filthy forehead and licked off the black residue—"chocolate?" Then

Miss Karnopolis ran—in the usual, frontward way—toward her home.

Miss Thistle came to just as she tackled the shirtless Mr. Bastable. "No! Bernard Bastable, why do you haunt me thus!" And she clambered off his rotund form and stormed home, cursing the moon.

Mrs. Havegood brushed chocolate crumbs from her dress. "Why are my clothes inside out?" she cried.

One by one, the rest of the multitude came to, shaking their heads in confusion, then politely tossing their paper plates into the trash cans and heading back to their houses, wondering how in God's name they'd ended up outside in the middle of the night covered in chocolate, and vowing never to speak about this event again.

By the time the last person had slunk from the square in shame, the sky had broken into a pale pink. The early morning sun glinted on the smattering of paper plates and plastic forks left on the brick plaza by those too disoriented to remember to throw them into the trash bins where they belonged.

Rose and Ty took a plastic garbage bag around the plaza and picked up.

"So, we're sure that did the trick, right?" Ty asked, looking exhausted.

Rose nodded. "Oh yeah. Definitely."

"Cool," Ty said, and he patted her on the back. "You know, I think Aunt Lily really digs me now. I'm glad I got to spend all this time with her. She's, like, *muy caliente.*"

"Good, I guess," Rose said, but it was the reverse of what she felt. As she walked away, she felt the sting of his words. Rose had assumed that she and her brothers were growing closer. Could she have been so wrong? *Were they just doing this for Lily the whole time?* she pondered. *Am I still invisible?*

As soon as Lily pulled the van back into the drive-way, Ty untied the speaker from the roof and dragged it onto the front porch, where Rose knew it would probably stay for months. Rose and Sage gathered all of the empty cake pans and carried them into the kitchen, where they found Mrs. Carlson sitting on the countertop, nervously chewing gum, her eyes wide and bloodshot and her hands shaking.

"Well!" she spat. "Look who decided to join us!"

Rose wasn't sure what she meant by *us* until she noticed Leigh running backward around the rolling countertop, still gurgling in backward English.

As if that weren't bad enough, Leigh had washed herself and combed her hair and put on a darling velvet tea party dress that Purdy bought her once for a wedding but which she'd refused to wear. Her Polaroid camera was nowhere to be found. In her backwardness, Leigh had transformed herself into a miniature pageant queen.

"She's been this way all night! I heard something that sounded like disco music in the distance, and I certainly would have gone, because disco music is the only thing that ever brought me any semblance of joy, but I couldn't leave the house, now could I? Not with our little spawn of *Satan* running around *backward*!"

Rose and Sage exchanged a cryptic glance, then dropped the dirty cake pans in the sink and ran out to the backyard.

"No! You can't leave again!" Mrs. Carlson cried out the door. "I haven't slept in a fortnight! I'm legally insane! I no longer hold myself responsible for my actions!"

Rose called out to Aunt Lily. "Leigh is still backward! We need more torte!"

But there was none left. The townspeople had eaten every slice. Even the cake pans themselves had been licked clean by the ravenous librarians.

Rose ran to the satellite dish, praying that there might be just a scrap of the batter left—she shouted with joy when she spotted a tiny pool of hardening batter in the very center, just enough for a torte the size of a silver dollar.

Rose scooped the batter out of the satellite dish

with a spoon and dropped it into a buttered white ramekin.

"You're baking?" Mrs. Carlson screamed at Rose as she pushed the ramekin into the oven. "Do you people do anything other than bake?"

Rose turned and looked Mrs. Carlson straight in her leathery Scottish face. "I'm sorry you got stuck here all night, I really am. But we were all dealing with some important business. And I have a funny feeling that right now all Leigh needs is just a little bit of chocolate cake. So please step aside."

Mrs. Carlson glared at Rose like she wanted to individually eat all of her fingers, but she backed away from the oven, and Rose cooked the batter for fifteen minutes until it was puffed and dark.

"Ghiel!" Rose called to her little sister, surprised at how adept she'd become at spinning words around in her head.

"Not you, too! Spawn of the devil!" shouted Mrs. Carlson.

Rose held the cake high above her prim and proper little sister's head. "On ekac rof uoy!" she admonished, which, of course, made Leigh desperate for the tiny chocolate bomb. She jumped high in the air and seized the plate from Rose, then gobbled up the cake and let out a little burp. Then she shook her head out, dazed, yawned grumpily, and marched upstairs to her bed—forward.

"What was in that cake?" Mrs. Carlson asked, audibly licking her lips.

Rose shrugged. "Sometimes a girl just needs some chocolate."

Mrs. Carlson harrumphed. "I am going to bed."

Aunt Lily piped in. "We are *all* going to bed. But first things first: We've got to open up the bakery in one hour—just to make sure everyone is back to normal."

Ty and Sage went upstairs with Leigh and Mrs. Carlson, but Aunt Lily held Rose back. "That was, in a word, sensational. Everyone in your family, Rose, is fine. Your parents, your brother, your baby sister, are fine. But you, you are sensational. You win the day."

Rose hugged her aunt and pondered things as she climbed the stairs. Sage was still annoying, and Ty was still aloof, but they *had* come together and formed a team, and that had meant more to her than any bit of praise or respect she'd ever gotten.

In the bathroom, Rose went to brush her teeth and looked in the mirror with shock. All of the makeup had worn off—the running around and baking and sweating must have done that. She was no longer glamorous.

Had the lipstick and the eye shadow still been there when she'd spoken to Devin? It was impossible to know. Aunt Lily had called her sensational. But staring into the mirror now, all Rose felt was ordinary.

And in that moment, she decided that she would rather be sensational than ordinary. She would do anything to feel like she felt today for the rest of her life.

Just about anything at all.

## CHAPTER 16
## *Sunrise, Sunset*

Rose woke up after only a half-hour of tossing and turning. She was too anxious for the day's events to really sleep. Today was like Christmas, only the present she was hoping for wasn't something new—she was praying that her magic had worked, and that everything would be just as it always had been: kind of boring.

Rose stared wide-eyed out her bedroom window. It

was only 7:30 a.m., but the sky already glowed a bright blue. Even the sun was anxious.

Rose decided that if even one person marched into the bakery backward that day, she would have to leave town forever. She would run to another town far away and get adopted by a lovely couple who couldn't have children of their own, and she would never tell them about her origins as a magical baker and how she had once ruined an entire town and then abandoned it like Victor Frankenstein abandoned his monster.

Not that she was under any pressure or anything.

While Rose gazed out the window, plotting her escape, she heard a knock at the front door. She bolted down the stairs into the front room, still in her rumpled jeans and striped T-shirt from the night before.

A man was rapping delicately on the glass door of the bakery.

After a moment of confused squinting, Rose recognized him as none other than Calamity Falls' premier acrobat and exotic dancer, Mr. Bastable.

His appearance was anything but normal. He wore a handsome burgundy sweater under an impeccably tailored gray blazer. He had obviously showered—recently!—because the white poofs of hair on either side of his head sparkled in the sun like fresh-picked cotton. When Rose opened the door, her nose was blasted with the smell of cologne.

Rose's heart almost stopped in her chest. It wasn't over yet—there was something wrong with Mr. Bastable. He was clean and pressed and dressed like a professor, or a newscaster. He looked positively dapper.

He was still backward.

But then Mr. Bastable said, in plain English, "Good morning, Rose," and she breathed a sigh of relief. His breath glowed with the smell of mint. What had gotten into Mr. Bastable? At least he hadn't called her Esor.

"Good morning, Mr. B . . . ," she answered warily.

"Please forgive me for coming so early. I'll need two carrot-bran muffins."

Rose peered at him with confusion. Mr. Bastable usually came in around 8:30 a.m., when the bakery officially opened, and he had never, in the decade Rose had known him, ordered more than one muffin. Rose reached under the glass counter for two carrot-bran muffins, plopped them in a white paper bag, and handed them to Mr. Bastable.

"Thank you," he said, and then he sat down on the wrought-iron bench outside the front window.

This was terribly strange, and made Rose think that perhaps the Back-to-Before Blackberry Torte had only half worked: Maybe it made people walk and speak normally but turned their routines upside down. Mr. Bastable always hurried away from the bakery as though his life depended on it. But there he was, sitting straight as a pole on the bench outside. He wasn't even eating his muffins.

At around eight a.m., Chip came into the shop and helped Rose prepare the bakery for the morning.

"Did I miss anything crazy last night?" he asked.

"Oh, no." *Just a townwide zombie disco party,* Rose thought.

Rose and Chip wiped down the glass-front case and the mosaic café tables and set new trays of muffins in place of older, stale ones. All the while, Mr. Bastable just sat on the bench. The sun grew hotter and she could see him dabbing at his forehead with a napkin. At one point he took off his blazer. But otherwise he didn't move, and he didn't eat either of his muffins. He just sat and waited.

At eight-thirty, when Rose flipped the sign on the front door to OPEN, Mr. Bastable was still waiting on the bench.

"What's he doing?" asked Aunt Lily from right behind her. Rose gasped and jumped.

"Oh, we're not sure," Rose answered.

Lily disappeared into the kitchen to help Chip while Ty joined Rose at the counter. A crowd of about ten had gathered outside the door.

"I think everyone is okay," Rose told Ty, who had put on a clean striped shirt and a pair of khakis. "They're walking normally, and they seem to be talking normally. There's just the curious case of Mr. Bastable. He hasn't moved in an hour."

"Is he waiting for someone?" asked Ty.

Rose didn't have time to answer as the crowd burst through the front door and formed a noisy line at the counter. Mrs. Havegood was first. She was wearing a loud red dress and a mink stole.

"Rose, dear, I need three dozen snickerdoodles, but real snickerdoodles this time."

"I'm sorry about that last batch, Mrs. Havegood," said Rose. "I know the Cambodian president must have been disappointed."

"Oh, he was indeed. We ordered pizza instead, and it turns out that he is lactose intolerant. He vowed never to visit me again, and I told him that was just fine. I am tired of entertaining foreign heads of state. They all have bizarre accents. You can't understand a thing they say. In any case, would you mind fetching me some regular snickerdoodles, Thyme?"

Ty flared his nostrils like a bull. "Not at all," he said, still upset with Mrs. Havegood for lying. He ducked into the kitchen.

Mrs. Havegood beckoned Rose in close as they waited for Ty to return with the cookies. "Come here, Rose. I'm going to tell you a truth," she whispered. "When you have all the money in the world, like I do, sometimes even that isn't enough. And you have to invent things that are even more fabulous than all your money. That is a truth."

Rose looked Mrs. Havegood straight in the eye and smiled. It was a startling admission from the biggest liar in town. Rose suddenly stopped hating Mrs. Havegood and saw her for what she was: lonely.

Ty returned with a white box filled with little tan snickerdoodles. "Here we are, Mrs. Havegood. So the real snickerdoodles are for . . . ?"

"Me and Jimmy Carter."

"Former U.S. president Jimmy Carter?" Ty scoffed, and Rose swallowed a laugh. At least Mrs. Havegood hadn't lost her sense of imagination entirely.

"Yes," she said. "Jimmy and I are not ashamed to say we love snickerdoodles *that* much."

Ty glared at Mrs. Havegood. He wasn't about to let her win this one. "Let me see him," Ty said. "Let me see Jimmy Carter."

Mrs. Havegood shook her head. "He's very shy."

"You're lying," said Ty, his voice growing louder. "You're a lying liar who lies about everything."

Rose cupped her palm over Ty's mouth. "Ty!" she said.

But it was too late. "Fine!" Mrs. Havegood cried. "Jimmy!" she called out the window. "Come in here, Jimmy!"

That's when former U.S. president Jimmy Carter walked into the Bliss bakery. He looked older than he had in Rose's textbooks, but that made sense, because he had been president a long time ago. A few thin clumps of white hair cascaded over either side of his head and stopped just above the collar of his denim cowboy shirt.

"Jimmy's dear sister was my college roommate." She winked at Rose. "And that's a truth."

Ty's jaw dropped as he handed the box of snickerdoodles to Jimmy Carter. "The United States of America thanks you for your service," the former president said, smiling.

Mrs. Havegood chuckled as she took his arm. "Have a lovely day, Rose! You too, Thyme!"

Ty winced. It was the ultimate burn.

That is, until Ashley Knob walked in. She was wearing a dress that a normal person might wear to a movie premiere. It was green and short and far too revealing to be appropriate for a high-school girl. She pranced up to the counter and said, "I'd like a scooped-out blueberry muffin, please."

Rose furrowed her eyebrows. "Scooped out?"

"Yeah. It's where you scoop most of the flesh of

the muffin out. Otherwise the muffin has too many carbs."

Rose thought that that really defeated the purpose of eating a muffin in the first place, but she snapped on a pair of surgical gloves and dove right in.

Ty should have been helping other customers, but instead he leaned over the counter and whispered in dulcet tones, "Hey, do you remember two days ago, when we kissed? Through the glass?"

Ashley pretended not to hear him.

"You kissed me!" he repeated, louder and more forcefully. "We *kissed*."

"Um, I don't kiss people who work in bakeries," she said, her nose so high in the air that the top of her head was practically brushing her back.

"But you said you *loved* me," Ty said, smiling devilishly.

"I'm, like, horrified right now and don't know what you're talking about. I mean, you're pretty hot and stuff, so, maybe if you worked at a hedge fund or you were a lawyer or something I would have kissed you, but here you are scooping out muffins, so, like, no."

"But don't you remember the crowd of girls and you clawed your way to the front just to try to kiss me, and—"

"Let it go, Ty," said Rose.

Ashley Knob grabbed her scooped-out muffin and huffed out, the hard platinum ringlets of her long hair whipping Ty in the cheek.

"She totally kissed me through the glass," he whispered. "I wasn't hallucinating that, right?"

"No, but she was."

Ty paced around behind the counter. "I don't even like her—I just want her to know that she was going crazy over me. I need to find a picture of us kissing. Do we have any security cameras outside?" Ty threw off his apron, and Rose knew that he was done helping at the bakery for the day.

Ty was back to his old tricks.

Rose craned her neck over the saloon doors and saw Sage and Leigh bouncing up on the lawn where the trampoline had been, while Mrs. Carlson sunned herself in a lawn chair. Rose pursed her lips. She was still the only one really dedicated to the bakery. Nothing had changed. Maybe Aunt Lily was right. Maybe they really were just fine.

The day passed without anything too bizarre happening.

Rose's mind would have been completely at ease had Mr. Bastable budged from the bench, but he hadn't. He was still sitting there, in the blazing July heat, still in his sweater, his blazer folded beside him, and he still hadn't touched the muffins.

Rose was peering out at Mr. Bastable and worrying mightily when Devin Stetson walked in.

His hair was gelled into an insouciant ramp that curved off the base of his forehead. His lips were pink and a little chapped. His milky skin was tanned.

Devin had never been to the bakery before. Why

now? Why today, after she'd had literally thirty minutes of sleep and two days' worth of grease and dirt caked in her bangs? Why couldn't he have really seen her last night, when he so feebly attempted to kiss her cheek by backing his scalp into her face?

Devin lingered by the front door as his mother and father, both clad in Hawaiian print shirts and visors and sunglasses, perused the glass counter.

"Do you have any Danishes?" asked Mrs. Stetson. Her eyes were buggy and bright. "Or is it just *Danish*? The plural of *Danish*, is it *Danish*, or *Danishi*? You know, is it like *sheep*, where the plural is *sheep*? Do you know what I mean?" Rose stopped staring at Devin long enough to realize that Mrs. Stetson was talking to her.

"I never thought about it. People usually just ask for one Danish."

Mr. Stetson laughed as he went to look at the cakes.

Devin stayed by the door and looked at the floor and at the ceiling and everywhere but at Rose's face.

Obviously he had no recollection of the night before. Not that it had been real anyway.

He caught her looking at him, and made a face and nodded toward his parents, as if to say, "Sorry about them, they're really embarrassing."

Rose nodded back to him, as if to say, "Mine are the same way."

Devin gradually drifted up to the counter and eventually found himself right across from Rose. Rose's face was burning and her mouth was dry.

"You always buy donuts from us, right?"

"I wouldn't say *always*, but sometimes, yes," she said.

"I'm Devin. Hi."

"I'm Rose. Hi," she squeaked. Her hands began to tremble, and she hid them behind her back. Devin Stetson was talking to her! Without the aid of an Upside-Down Cake!

Rose smiled to herself while she packed up the Danish. Danishes? Pastries. She packed up the pastries.

"Thank you, dear!" yelled Mr. and Mrs. Stetson as they bustled out in their Hawaiian shirts.

Devin nodded in her direction. "See you around— like a donut," he said.

And Rose gave him a military salute, which she realized one second later was the single least attractive thing she could have done.

Rose was hating herself when she caught the reflection of Devin's face in the glass, wincing at his own lame pun.

Even though he didn't remember dancing with her, Rose had managed to jump the biggest hurdle of all: telling him her name. She smiled wider than she thought possible.

That is, until Miss Thistle approached the bakery, and Rose realized what had been keeping Mr. Bastable glued to that godforsaken bench all day. He'd been waiting for her.

Felidia Thistle was hurrying up to the front door in a breezy summer cotton dress, when she was stopped by the froglike squeak of Mr. Bastable.

"Wait!" he coughed. He tried again a moment later, clearer this time. "Wait. Miss Thistle."

Rose watched through the glass as Miss Thistle spun around, shocked. Apparently, she didn't remember any of the week's events, because she was smiling at Mr. Bastable, who looked truly handsome, despite the formidable sweat stains in his armpits.

"Miss Thistle, those wing nuts in the bakery gave me two carrot-bran muffins by mistake. Would you mind eating the other one? If I have too much starch, it activates my irritable bowel syndrome."

Rose winced. It could have been a lovely moment, save for the mention of irritable bowel syndrome.

But Miss Thistle didn't seem to mind. She sat down on the bench next to Mr. Bastable, and they slowly nibbled on their carrot-bran muffins, smiling at each other the entire time. Rose couldn't hear what they were saying—probably they were talking about science—but it was a start. She didn't even mind that

Mr. Bastable had called her a wing nut.

There was a magic in the two of them sitting there as the brilliant orange of the setting sun glimmered through the trees, but it had nothing to do with spells or mason jars. It was the magic of a person's ability to change, to grow, to heal, without the aid of any magic at all.

At the end of the day, after Chip had gone home and Mrs. Carlson had gone to bed, Rose sat in the booth in the kitchen and drank a glass of water, while looking out the backdoor window at her brothers. They were taking turns pushing Leigh on the swing set with such abandon that they nearly sent her flying over the top bar. It was nice to watch, but Rose still felt a little left out.

Aunt Lily sidled up to the kitchen table in an old-fashioned silk dressing gown covered in bright orange lilies.

"Rose, we need to talk. I have a proposition. You

know what I think of you and your potential. I think you should come to New York with me."

Rose blushed and laughed out loud. The thought of going to New York was so grand and so overwhelming that it sounded like a joke. "What for?"

"I want you to work on my TV show. At first you'll stay behind the scenes, helping me prepare recipes and figuring out how to teach them to a TV audience. But after a while I hope you'll join me on camera! I'll do your makeup, and we can be stars together! You have such gifts, gifts that far exceed operating a small business. We're a lot alike, you and I, and I want you to dream big. You're sensational, never forget that."

Rose imagined herself baking alongside Aunt Lily in the kitchen of a vast, gorgeous, city bakery, or on the soundstage of a TV studio in front of a live audience of laughing and doting fans. Oh, the love she would feel! The warmth, the acceptance, and the respect!

The thing in the basement had been right all along. Rose did desire beauty and importance, but she didn't want to drink them from a bottle labeled TINCTURE OF VENUS—she wanted to earn them. Maybe she would earn them on Lily's coattails, just like it had said.

Rose had to purse her lips together to contain her embarrassingly long smile. "But where would the recipes come from?"

"Well, that's the only little snag. We'd need the Bliss Cookery Booke. I've gathered a few magical recipes from the Bliss canon in my travels, but only enough for a few episodes."

"So you want to . . . steal the cookbook?"

Aunt Lily chuckled nervously. "No, of course not, dear. I'd only borrow it!"

"But won't my parents notice it's gone? How would they do their own baking?" And then she thought of something else she was almost afraid to ask. "Wouldn't they miss me?"

Aunt Lily pointed her finger and wiggled Rose's nose back and forth. "That, my darling, is the simple part. When I was young, I learned a recipe for a wonderful little treat called a Forget-Me Biscuit. You just whisper the name of the thing you'd like the eaters to forget—in our case, that would be you and me and the Bliss Cookery Booke—and you mix the whisper into the biscuit dough. Then we'd feed the biscuits to Ty, Sage, Leigh, Chip, Mrs. Carlson, and your mother and father, and then they'd forget that you or I or the book ever existed. They won't miss you a wink! They'll go on running a lovely bakery with their other lovely children—it just won't be magical. Meanwhile, you and I will become blisteringly, mind-blowingly famous and respected and adored!"

Rose couldn't believe she was even entertaining this notion, but there she was, entertaining it. "Do the biscuits really work?" she found herself asking.

"Oh, I know they work. I've used them before," Lily said, grinning. "How do you think I escaped my own humdrum family? I was destined for greatness, and they were only holding me back. So I whipped up a batch of biscuits, and they never got in my way again!"

Rose glanced outside again at her brothers as they pushed her sister back and forth in the swing. How could she leave them? Would their lives be the same without her?

On the other hand, how could she stay and let things go back to the way they had been? Rose couldn't take another day of being sent out like an errand girl to buy fruit while her parents did all the magic and her siblings all had better things to do. Not after this week. She'd seen the book in all its glory, and she wasn't about to give it up now. Still, the whole thing seemed a little drastic.

"I don't know if I can," said Rose.

"Well, it's just a matter of whether you'd like to stay here for the rest of your life and squander your gifts, or whether you want to really make something of yourself, to win the respect of millions and grow up to be a glamorous woman of the world. Like *moi*."

A glamorous woman of the world. Respected by

millions. Those were all that Rose ever wanted to be. But at what price?

"When would we leave?" Rose coughed. "*If* I were going."

Aunt Lily yawned nonchalantly. "Tomorrow morning. I will be up late preparing the dough for the Forget-Me Biscuits. If you'd like to go, join me in the kitchen late tonight and we'll make magic—"

Just as Aunt Lily was finishing up her instructions, Ty and Sage carried Leigh into the kitchen and settled into the booth with Lily and Rose.

Sage stood next to the table and made a proclamation. "I say we order *pizza* for dinner!" He bowed with one hand in front of him, as if he were wearing a cape. "This is our last night before Mom and Dad come back, and there will be no more fun food after that. And no more magic."

"Right. No more magic," Rose said. So it was true. Even Sage thought it. They would never be allowed to touch the cookbook again, even if they didn't mention all the trouble it had caused. Rose's parents just didn't trust her.

After Leigh fell asleep that night, Rose quietly packed her clothes.and her alarm clock into the little yellow duffel bag she sometimes brought to sleepovers. Then Rose tiptoed through the hallway and downstairs into the kitchen, where Aunt Lily was standing over the kitchen counter, an empty blue mason jar in her hand.

"Lily," her aunt whispered into the jar. The whisper glowed a faint purple as it swirled into the jar. Inside, the glowing air congealed into a faint ghostly image of Lily's smiling face.

Thankfully, Aunt Lily hadn't seen her. Rose continued watching.

"The Bliss Cookery Booke," Lily whispered. And the new whisper floated into the jar and formed an image of the familiar brown leather cover of the Cookery Booke.

And then, "Rosemary." When Aunt Lily whispered

her name, Rose's arms instantly broke out into cold, clammy goose bumps.

Rose watched as Lily's whisper formed a glowing image of Rose's whole body inside the jar. She couldn't say for sure, but it looked from her perch on the steps like her image was banging on the glass walls of the jar, screaming to be let out.

Aunt Lily screwed the top on the mason jar and shook it, then opened it over a metal mixing bowl in which she'd prepared a crumbly, buttery dough. The whispers whipped out of the jar and into the bowl. The ball of dough rose out of the bowl and shattered into a thousand little pieces that hung suspended in the hot, dark air of the kitchen.

The crumbles of dough swirled around, slowly at first, then faster, like leaves in an eddy, until all the minuscule pieces swirled back into the bowl like they were going down a drain.

Aunt Lily patted the dough with her hands. "All right! That's done."

That's when she looked up and noticed Rose standing on the stairs.

Aunt Lily smiled widely. They both knew what this meant.

"I'm coming to New York," Rose whispered.

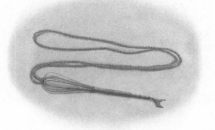

## CHAPTER 17
## *Homecoming*

*B*efore the crack of dawn the next morning, Aunt Lily went to Rose's room and shook her awake. "Let's go, my darling! The biscuits are baking downstairs."

Rose slipped on a pair of jeans and a blue T-shirt that she'd laid out for the trip. Then, once Aunt Lily had disappeared downstairs, Rose slipped into the bathroom to brush her teeth one final time.

Rose was surprised to see Ty and Sage and Leigh inside, having a brush party. Ty looked annoyingly handsome as ever in his navy basketball shorts. Sage's hair was a wild curly mess. Leigh stared up at Rose with dark, trusting eyes that seemed to take up the entire upper half of her face. It had been easier to imagine being away from them the night before, when they weren't right in front of her, looking so earnest.

"What are you guys doing up so early?"

"We're gonna make breakfast for Mom and Dad when they come home," said Sage.

"Will you help us?" asked Ty. "We don't actually know how to make anything."

Leigh ran up to Rose and tugged on the leg of her jeans. "Look what I found, Rosie!" Rose looked down and saw Leigh clutching her old Polaroid camera.

"Why do you have that?" Rose asked.

"I wanna picture!" Leigh said, her eyes wide and her voice high and squeaky. She pointed at Rose and her brothers.

"Come in for a picture, *mi hermana*," said Ty. And he put one arm around Rose and another around Sage, and then Rose picked up Leigh and held her close, the camera turned around in her hands so that it was aimed at the four of them. There was a flash as Leigh snapped a photo.

Sage blew on the picture when it fell out of the camera and handed it to Leigh. Everyone leaned in to watch the picture develop.

After a minute, the images of Rose and her siblings came to life on paper: Ty standing tall with his spiky red hair; Sage, pudgy, with his curly orange hair; Leigh, whose mouth was wide-open; and Rose, with her long dark hair, the black sheep.

"I'm going to keep this one," Rose told her sister. She took the picture and stuffed it in the pocket of her shirt, right over her heart.

"Why are you crying, Rose?" Sage asked. "You don't look *that* bad in the picture."

Rose wiped a salty tear from her cheek. "I just . . .

I love you guys, is all."

Ty and Sage looked at Rose like she had five heads. Leigh just hugged her big sister's leg.

"I mean, we love you too, Rosita," said Ty. "Duh! That goes without saying!"

Rose peeled off her sister and ran from the bathroom. She couldn't stand to look at their faces anymore.

"Where are you going, weirdo?" Sage yelled. "What is wrong with girls?"

"I'll be right back!" Rose shouted from the top of the stairs. But she wouldn't be right back. At least they wouldn't have to miss her.

Downstairs she found Aunt Lily, who had baked the biscuits and arranged them in a picnic basket on the table with a note that said, "Please Eat."

"Ready?" said Aunt Lily eagerly. Her hair was glossy and clean and dark like Rose's own, and her dress was white with tiny colored flowers along the hem.

"Sure am." Rose nodded gravely. She pulled the Polaroid picture of her and her family from her pocket and looked at it.

"Isn't that darling?" Aunt Lily said, leaning over her shoulder. And then she slid the picture from Rose's fingers and placed it in the trash.

"Why did you do that?" Rose asked, furious.

"I can't let you take any pictures with you, Rose. They mess with the magic of the Forget-Me Biscuits. If you look at a picture of someone who has eaten the biscuit, they'll be able to remember you. And that would be very painful for them, because then they'll know you're gone. So I'm sorry, but it's got to be a clean break. You'll have to leave your pictures. It's best for everyone."

And with that, Aunt Lily picked up her little tweed suitcase and stepped out the back door. "Coming, darling?"

Rose looked at Aunt Lily, her chic haircut, her painted lips, the arch of her perfect eyebrows. Then an impatience flashed through Aunt Lily's eyes—the same impatience that had made Rose pause so many times before trusting Aunt Lily with the truth.

Rose hadn't planned on tossing the Forget-Me Biscuits in the garbage, but that's exactly what she did. It was as if her hands were working quite on their own. Rose reached beneath the steaming pile of trashed biscuits, pulled out the Polaroid, and stuffed it back into her pocket.

"No!" Aunt Lily cried. "What are you doing?"

"I'm sorry, Aunt Lily," Rose said quietly. "But I just can't leave my family. They're not perfect, not by a long shot, but I can't steal the cookbook and run away. It's not right. And even if they ate these biscuits and never thought about me, I'd be thinking about them the whole time. What's the point of being famous if the people who love you most don't even know you anymore?"

Rose took the first deep breath she'd taken in a week. There, at last, was the truth of the matter.

Aunt Lily was fuming. She had lost all her cool. Rose had never seen her crack anything but a smile— now her skin had gone all red, and the corners of her mouth turned down into an angry, ugly growl. "But they don't appreciate you! When your parents get back, they'll lock up the book and they won't let you bake anything, and your brothers will go back to ignoring you! They don't love you, Rose; *I* love you."

"You don't even know who I am."

"What do you mean?" Aunt Lily shouted. "Of course I know who you are!"

"You've known me one week. If you loved me, you'd have been here from the beginning. You'd have stuck with me, like my parents and my brothers have. You wouldn't just come around when they're gone to try to steal our cookbook."

Lily didn't even try to argue that one. Rose finally saw the truth. Lily had come for the book.

"If you come with me, you'll be famous. You'll be glamorous. People will look up to you. I'll teach you all the tricks! You think boys like Devin Stetson will fawn all over you when they're not under a magical stupor?" Aunt Lily wagged her finger. "Wrong. You need me, Rose. Without me you're nothing."

Rose's nose wrinkled in disgust. Something snapped into place inside of Rose. Aunt Lily wasn't the strong, independent woman Rose had imagined her to be. Aunt Lily was the weak one. Maybe Devin Stetson wouldn't like her without any makeup. Maybe her parents wouldn't let her bake magical recipes once they were back home.

But at least they loved her.

Aunt Lily loved only herself.

"Actually, Aunt Lily, I'm doing just fine." Rose said. "You're the one who has nothing." Rose held out her open palm. "Now, give me the key."

With a sneer, Lily removed the key from around her neck and plopped it into Rose's outstretched hand. "Knock yourself out," she said coldly.

And then Aunt Lily hitched her tweed suitcase to

her motorcycle and sped away.

At the roar of Lily's motor and the sound of squealing tires, Ty and Sage hurried downstairs with Leigh. "Did Aunt Lily just go?" Sage asked. "Why didn't she say good-bye?"

"She was in a hurry," said Rose. She couldn't help but smile. Then she put an arm around both of her brothers, stared down at Leigh, and said, "Now let's go make that breakfast."

Half an hour after Aunt Lily left, a caravan of black armored cars pulled into the driveway, and Purdy's high soprano rang out from the driveway like a Christmas bell. "Kiddles! We're home! Remember us?"

Albert and Purdy burst through the backdoor into the kitchen, and Leigh jumped and giggled and catapulted herself into her father's outstretched arms.

Purdy pulled Rose to her chest and kissed the top of her head. As soon as Rose felt the softness of her mother's cotton robes, the wild curls of her hair, the smells of honey and flour and grease on her soft skin, Rose couldn't believe that she had thought even for one second that she could ever leave her family. That she could ever live without them. And she swore to herself that she would never tell a soul that she had agreed—for a moment!—to go with Aunt Lily.

"Ooh, I love you, I love you!" said Purdy, kissing Rose over and over again on the forehead like a hungry woodpecker on a tree.

Albert put down Leigh and hugged Sage and Ty close. "My boys!" he said.

Mrs. Carlson came down the stairs carrying her suitcase and looking a few decades older than she had when she'd first arrived. "Well! Thank goodness you're back! It's a miracle I'm still alive! I'm still exhausted from all their antics!" Mrs. Carlson pushed through the saloon doors and shouted back into the kitchen. "You have very bizarre children! But then again, this is a very bizarre town! I'm moving back to Glasgow, where no one speaks backward! Ever!"

Purdy looked at Rose quizzically. "What's she talking about?"

"Oh, she's just kidding around."

Rose then realized that Janice Hammer had been standing in the kitchen the whole time, looking severely at the loving family with her arms folded across her chest.

Then she proclaimed, "Your parents are heroes!"

Sage jumped up and down. "Did you cure the flu?" he asked.

Mayor Hammer cleared her throat. "They not only cured the flu, they also cured a few cases of short-term memory loss and some broken hearts as well. It was as if the croissants were magic!" She barked out a nervous laugh that startled everyone. "Magic! Ha! But those croissants did have a certain effectiveness that seemed . . . otherworldly." Mayor Hammer pulled herself back to reality. "And that's why we gave them the key to the city."

Albert triumphantly held up the thing hanging

around his neck, which was a two-foot-long cardboard cutout of a yellow key wrapped in red ribbon.

"What does it open?" Sage asked excitedly. "City Hall? Can we have a party in there?"

Mayor Hammer blinked at Sage. "It doesn't open anything! It's a symbol of our gratitude and respect."

Sage harrumphed. "Respect, huh? Respect is one thing. Me having my circus-themed tenth birthday party in your city hall is another."

Purdy broke the tension by turning to her children and lilting, "So! How did everything go?"

Rose opened her mouth to answer, but Mayor Hammer cut in before she could make a sound. "Well, that's my cue. I don't want to hear about your family. I mean—I don't want to *intrude* on your family."

She bowed to Albert and Purdy and said, "Thank you for everything. Truly." Then she hustled into her black Hummer, rolled up the tinted window, and sped away with her caravan of armored cars.

Rose rolled her eyes. "Was she like that the entire time?"

"Worse," Albert said, smiling. "Now, answer your mother's question, kiddles: How did the week go?"

Rose looked desperately at Ty and Sage, and found that they were looking desperately at her in return. It was obvious that they couldn't share the truth with their parents, but they had forgotten to come up with a lie.

"Oh, it all went smoothly," Rose said, trying to come up with something on the fly. "Chip was wonderful. Mrs. Carlson was very nice to us. Nothing out of the ordinary."

Purdy smiled and waited, pushing her floppy mane of black curls out of her face. Albert stood in the background, his fair, red-haired arms crossed over his thin chest. "That's it?" she said. "Tell me the good stuff! Who baked what? Did any customers place special orders?"

Rose was about the settle the matter by shaking her

head "no" when Ty interrupted.

"Umm, I baked all the muffins," he said, words spilling out of his mouth like vomit. "I . . . invented new muffins. They were giant muffins. I baked two giant muffins the size of basketballs and I sliced them like a cake and people told me that I had invented a new genre of baked goods called the muffin cake and . . . I got a prize."

And Rose learned something new about her brother: He was the worst liar she had ever seen.

"A prize?" said Albert skeptically.

"From me," said Rose, trying desperately to cut him off before something truly crazy came out of Ty's mouth. Why couldn't he have just said something normal? "I gave him the prize of my . . . sisterhood."

And then Sage made things worse. "And I baked a cheesecake! It was an . . . onion cheesecake, and everyone thought it was gonna be gross but they loved it so much that I got a bigger prize than Ty!"

Albert and Purdy squinted at him and didn't say

anything, which only seemed to egg him on more. "Also someone ordered a wedding cake in the shape of a shark, and I made it, and we drove two hours to the beach to deliver it!" Sage snapped his jaws shut a few times. "A shark!" he repeated.

Albert was starting to grow angry wrinkles at the corners of his eyes. "You drove? Which of my unlicensed children drove a car?"

Rose thought quickly. "Oh, don't worry, it was Chip."

"No!" Sage cut in. "It was Ty. He drove the car with his learner's permit."

Ty swatted Sage in the back of the head.

"Ty, is that true?" said Albert.

Ty just stared into space like a scared squirrel, not knowing which way to turn.

Albert and Purdy looked at each other, then Purdy slumped against the chopping-block table. "Okay. We know that you are all lying," she said, "if for no other reason than there has never been a request for a shark-shaped wedding cake in the history of wedding cakes. Now, what really happened?"

Rose was about to explain that there had been a little trouble with the cookbook but that Aunt Lily had helped them fix it, but as soon as she conjured the image of Aunt Lily's tall frame and big hips and short hair and delicate nose in her head, Rose found that her tongue again went limp. Just like a few days before.

Rose tried to say the words *Aunt Lily*, but it sounded instead like she was trying to cough out a hairball. The boys were clearly experiencing the same problem, as they both stood there making hacking noises.

"What's wrong?" Albert said. "Why can't you talk?"

Purdy gasped. "Oh my goodness. Albert, doesn't it look like they've eaten a Hold-Your-Tongue Tart?"

Albert thought frantically for a moment, then said, "You're right! But who could have given them a Hold-Your-Tongue Tart? And why?"

Rose was confused. A Hold-Your-Tongue tart?

Could that be another name for any of the recipes they'd made that week? Not that it would matter—Rose and her brothers hadn't actually eaten any of the baked goods they made.

Then Rose remembered the shimmering, rainbow-colored tart that Lily had made for them her first night there, how they'd all thought it was the most delicious thing they'd ever tasted, and how after eating it, Ty had been too tongue-tied on the phone with their parents to mention Aunt Lily. Had that shimmering little slice rendered them unable to mention its maker?

Figures. If Lily had come there in order to take the book, of course she would have done something drastic to keep Albert and Purdy from knowing she was there.

Rose tried to ask about the tart, but it came out all wrong. "We ate a tart—made by—" and then her tongue grew fat and heavy and she could no longer speak.

Albert and Purdy were chattering frantically when

Rose remembered that Leigh hadn't eaten more than a tiny nibble of the tart.

She stooped down, gathered Leigh into her arms, and said, "Leigh, tell Mom and Dad who visited us this week!"

Leigh thought a minute, putting a grubby finger to her lips, then remembered. "Aunt Lily!" she proclaimed.

Albert and Purdy went silent. There was a frantic look in their eyes that Rose had never seen before. It was terrifying.

"*Lily* was here?" Purdy asked, spitting out the name like it was something putrid and ugly. She made fists with her hands.

Rose and Ty and Sage nodded quickly.

"Did she feed you a tart that shimmered like the scales of a fish and the iridescent neck of a mallard duck?" asked Albert, his eyes open so wide the lashes practically touched his forehead.

Rose nodded again. That was exactly what they'd eaten.

"Why did you let her in?" Purdy asked, exasperated.

Rose tried to explain. "She—said—" but she couldn't form the words. Rose pointed to her own shoulder blade, then lifted her pant leg a little bit and pointed to the ladle-shaped birthmark on her calf.

"Did Lily show you her ladle birthmark to fool you into thinking that she's part of our family?" said Albert.

Rose nodded a third time.

"Wait—she's *not* part of our family?" Sage asked, his voice aching with disappointment and fury, like he was being told for the first time that the Tooth Fairy wasn't real.

"Well, *technically* she's part of our family," said Purdy, pacing back and forth angrily. "But she's from the side of the family that we don't talk about."

"The Albatross side?" blurted out Ty.

"Yes," said Purdy. "Their side is a tricky bunch. I know Lily because she came here years ago, when Ty was a baby, and she tried to steal the Bliss Cookery Booke."

Rose shook her head in disgust. "Blech—" Rose coughed. She still couldn't say Lily's name. "She claimed didn't know about the book!"

"Well, not until we showed it to her!" said Sage. "She loved it!"

Purdy gasped like she'd been punched in the stomach. "You *showed* her the book? How *could* you?"

Rose felt her eyes well up. It felt like the bottom had fallen out of the world and she was still there, floating in a gelatinous goop of terror and shame. *At least I didn't run away with her,* she wanted to say. *At least I got her to leave, and the book is still here and safe.*

Then Rose's tongue got its groove back. It was as if the pain of disappointing her mother had released the tart's icy hold.

"L . . . ll . . . llll . . . llll . . . ily!" she managed. "Aunt Lily!"

After a moment of extreme concentration, suddenly Sage and Ty could say it out loud too: "Lily!"

Apparently the Hold-Your-Tongue Tart had a

loophole: extreme, all-consuming fear.

Sage began to explain why they had shown the book to Aunt Lily in the first place. "Aunt Lily would never steal anything!" he screamed. "Aunt Lily is the most beautiful, interesting, helpful, fantastical person we have ever met! She wanted to see the book because she wanted to help us fix the town! If it weren't for her, everyone would still be walking backward!"

Albert narrowed his gaze. "And just *why* were they walking backward?"

Then Sage spilled the whole story from start to finish. It was confusing, but their parents didn't seem too interested in the details. When Sage was done, he smiled and sketched a little bow, as if he's just finished the showstopping number in a huge, lavish musical.

But life was not a musical, of course.

Rose couldn't remember ever having felt worse in her entire life. She was speechless.

"That woman is very dangerous," Purdy said slowly. "My gosh, what has gotten into you children?"

She glanced around the room as though she had never seen them before, as though this were not her home.

"But she's so nice and pretty!" Ty protested.

Albert stopped his puffing for a moment to chime in. "The scariest ones always are," he said. "That's a life lesson, Son."

Purdy pressed her fists against her temples. "Enough of this. Where is she? And where is the cookbook?"

"Rose?" said Albert, not hiding his frown. "May we have the copy of the key we gave to you, please?"

"Don't worry, Dad. She's gone. I have the key."

"And is the book safe?" Purdy and Albert asked simultaneously.

"There's only one way to find out," Rose said, fishing out of her pocket the little silver whisk that Lily had given back.

Rose shivered as she moved through the frigid corridor—not from the cold, but from the realization that her gut been right all along: Aunt Lily was a shady character. She thanked goodness that she'd turned down Aunt Lily's offer and had the presence to take back the key before her aunt could steal the cookbook.

Rose pulled back the green tapestry, put the key into the lock, and turned. Albert, Purdy, Ty, Sage, and Leigh looked on from behind her. She yanked the chain on the overhead bulb. The podium was empty, except for a small cream-colored envelope.

The book was gone.

Rose felt her knees go out and heard her mother screaming her name, as if from a mile away, under water. Rose didn't remember what happened after that.

## CHAPTER 18

# Disappearing Acts

*R*ose woke up in her bed with Leigh bouncing up and down next to her. She looked up and saw her mother and father and Ty and Sage staring down, worried. There was a wet towel on her forehead.

"What happened?" Rose whispered.

"You fainted, honey," said Purdy, her face washed with concern. "You swooned like a Victorian woman in a melodrama."

"Where is the Cookery Booke?" Rose panted, try-ing to sit up.

Albert gently pushed her shoulders back to the pil-low. "Just rest, sweetheart," he said. "The book is gone. She left us a *letter* in exchange."

"What does it say?" Rose asked. She prayed it didn't mention her almost betrayal.

"We haven't read it yet. There was the matter of you collapsing on the floor, darling, and that took precedence." Albert pulled a piece of scented off-white stationery from the little envelope Rose had spotted on the podium. He unfolded it, cleared his throat, and began to read aloud:

*Dearest Fourth Cousin Purdy and Family,*

*As I'm sure you've noticed by now, I have taken the Bliss Cookery Booke. I have not done this out of spite for you or any of your remarkable and lovely children, but because*

I felt that your claim to the book has expired.
Ever since our great-great-great-grandfathers
Filbert and Albatross had their little tiff, the
Cookery Booke has filtered down through the
generations on your side of the family, yet you
have done nothing with it but squander its power
by running popular local businesses in small,
eccentric towns. As I believe I am better
equipped to tap into the book's full economic and
political potential, I took it.

Please do not let whatever preconceptions
you have about the Albatross genealogy worry
you. I am not a nefarious creature like the rest of
my family. I will use these recipes to help those
who cannot help themselves by broadcasting
them on what is sure to be my wildly successful
cable TV cooking show. I'm sure you'll be
doing the world a greater service by allowing
me to share these priceless recipes rather than
keeping them cooped up in your refrigerator and

*leaving your children with the overwhelming responsibility of guarding them.*

*Look out for me on television!*

*Love and kisses,*
*Aunt Lily*

"And then she kissed the paper," said Albert, turning the page around to reveal a lipstick imprint of Lily's mouth.

"That selfish, manipulative coward!" Purdy exclaimed, her hands balling into tiny fists. "That side of the family just spawned one bad seed after another."

"I can't believe this," Ty whined, folding his arms across his chest. "How are we supposed to run the bakery without that cookbook?"

"That's not even our biggest problem," said Albert, rubbing his temples in tiny circles. "What if she decides to broadcast some of the more destructive recipes in that book? What if she unleashes the craziness of Albatross's Apocrypha onto America? We could have whole towns, whole cities overrun with chaos! The country could be ruined!"

Rose pulled the sheet over her head and groaned, then began to weep. "Mama," she said. "Papa. I'm sorry I made such a mess. It's all because I wanted to show you that I could be a magical baker. So you'd respect me. I tried to do everything right. But I did everything wrong."

Purdy pulled the sheet back from Rose's face and kissed her cheek. "Honey, we *do* respect you. You're the most clever and talented person in this family. We know we make a big deal about Ty being so handsome and Sage being funny and Leigh being adorable, and sometimes we leave you out of the mix, but the truth is that this family would fall apart without you."

Albert nodded. Ty patted Rose's knee. Leigh nuzzled into Rose's cheek.

Sage bounced in place, a pained expression on his face. "Can we eat breakfast now?"

Rose couldn't help it—she started to laugh. Harder than she had laughed all summer. Her parents loved and respected her. Deep down, she supposed she'd always known that. But sometimes—like now—it was important just to hear it.

"Of course we can, Sage," Rose said, sitting up. "Of course we can."

Downstairs in the kitchen, Sage saw the dozen or so biscuits in the garbage can. "Whoa, biscuits! Can we eat these?" he asked.

"No!" Rose shouted. "They were . . . bad."

Rose watched as Purdy fetched a carton of eggs from the refrigerator, Albert bounced Leigh up and down on his knee, and Ty and Sage swatted at one another in a fake karate fight. Purdy's hair was frizzed and wild, Albert's socks were long and dingy, Leigh's clean shirt already looked like she'd worn it eight days in a row, Ty was as vain as Ashley Knob, and Sage was all-around ridiculous.

Mrs. Carlson was right. They were a bizarre family.

And a family was something that Aunt Lily would never have, because she'd given hers up a long time ago. And that's why Lily was vulnerable: She was alone.

"Hey, guys," Rose said, staring out at the tire tracks that Lily's motorcycle had left in the driveway.

"What, *mi hermana?*" Ty asked. The entire Bliss family turned to look at Rose. Her family would do anything for her. And she would do anything for them. She knew what she had to do—with their help, of course.

"I'm going to get our cookbook back."

"All in good time, dear. All in good time." Purdy smacked her hands clean on a towel. "But first, you need something to eat. No one ever did anything great on an empty stomach."

So Rose turned away from the door and joined her family at the kitchen table, where Purdy set down a plate of scrambled eggs. As Rose gobbled them up, she listened to her family talk and laugh over one another's stories, and even after Chip came in to open the shop, they all stayed glued to the table. It dawned on Rose, sitting there in that hot, cramped kitchen, that she was truly happy.

# Acknowledgments

Thank you to the following magicians:

Katherine Tegen, for believing in this novel and helping to bring it to life; Katie Bignell for all of her assistance; and everyone at HarperCollins Children's Books for pulling it all together, and for believing in the Bliss Family.

Alexandra Carillo-Vaccino, Cara Kilduff, Nora Salzman, Jordan Barbour, and Tony Rodriguez, for years of support, generosity, and laughter.

The folks at the finest bakery in the world, Les Ambassades, for their warm smiles and their addictive, perfect croissants.

My funny and brilliant mother and sister, both incredible writers—not many people get to be as genuinely proud of their family as I am of you.

JAG, whose constant support, kindness, and devotion have officially qualified me as the luckiest.

And finally, at the Inkhouse:

Michael Stearns for his wise editorial guidance and for giving me this incredible opportunity.

And Ted Malawer, whose ambition and talent always inspire me to push myself further, whose generosity has rescued me in so many ways, and whose jokes always make me laugh. You are a once-in-a-lifetime friend.